A Yearning Dilemma

DENISE CARBO

Copyright © 2022 by Denise Carbo

All rights reserved.

No part of this book may be reproduced in any form or by any electronic or mechanical means, including information storage and retrieval systems, without written permission from the author, except for the use of brief quotations in a book review.

❦ Created with Vellum

For my future daughter-in-law, Ashley. You're already a cherished member of our family! Your sunny demeanor and kindness are a gift!

Chapter One

The door opens and my stomach plummets to my toes like I'm on a rollercoaster plunging down a terrifying drop.

What is he doing here?

Has he tracked me down after all this time?

No, that's not realistic. Is it?

He tilts back his black cowboy hat. Blond hair, the exact color of freshly made waffles, brushes his forehead. He holds a phone to his ear with a scowl on his too handsome face. A face that's been featured in multiple blockbuster movies over the past decade—not that I've seen a single one. If Holden Fox is in a movie, then I skip the movie.

"The answer is no. There's nothing to discuss." His gaze sweeps my store and lands on me. "I've got to hang."

My heart pounds in my ears and my throat is as dry as a desert. A sharp pinch stabs my finger.

Bollocks! I've stabbed myself with the needle. A drop of blood forms, and I stick my finger in my mouth before the blood can stain the fabric. How would I explain to Mrs. Roberts I ruined her blouse because I was too busy staring at Holden Fox?

"Is this the only store in town called Dress to Impress? Wait, this is Granite Cove, right?" He frowns down at his phone. "Did my GPS send me somewhere else?"

So he's not lost.

"You're in Granite Cove, and this is the only dress shop in town. Let alone the only one called Dress to Impress. I'm Kelly Tanner, the owner."

His gaze swings up to mine without a trace of recognition.

Of course he doesn't remember me. I was nothing but a momentary distraction to him.

Good, it's better this way.

He swaggers over to the counter in faded jeans and a tarnished, dented belt buckle.

"I was told to come here for my fitting, but it must be a mistake." His green gaze narrows as he scans the racks of clothes filling the store. He checks his phone and scowls.

The low, Texas drawl sends a shot of heat through my core, but I dump an enormous pitcher of ice on my traitorous hormones and grit my teeth.

Fitting? Please no. Fate couldn't be that cruel.

"H.A.? Mitch and Franny's wedding?" I hold my breath. Please say no.

"Yeah."

Why didn't Franny warn me? A simple heads-up Mitch's best man is a famous actor isn't too much to expect, is it?

"Then you're in the right place."

He looks around my store again and frowns.

Seriously, dude? My shop may not be the swanky, Rodeo Drive type of places he must be used to, but it's not some crappy hole-in-the-wall, either.

"If you'll follow me, I'll show you to a fitting room where you can try on the tux." I stalk around the counter toward the back of the store. Why did I tell Lenore she could have the day off today? I could be safely hidden in the backroom right now and leave her to deal with Mr. Hotshot Celebrity Too Good for My Small-Town Store. She may have never actually measured or fitted any of my wedding clients before, but I have trained her how. So what if this is the highest profile wedding I've ever done?

I snatch back the curtain on the dressing room I reserve for brides to accommodate the large trains or skirts and wave him in with a tight smile. "I'll bring out your tux."

A spicy scent reaches my nose as he glides past me and tosses his hat on the small table in the corner. I swivel away and stride to the backroom. What the heck does the A stand for? Arrogant? Ass? Actor? If Franny had said H.F. I might have put two and two together. Then again, probably not. It never occurred to me Franny's famous husband might have an equally famous best man. It should have.

I grab the tux and fold it over my arm. She could have warned me. When she handed over the measurements and said the best man couldn't arrive until right before the wedding, I should have asked more questions. Simply ensuring a qualified tailor took the measurements wasn't enough. I would have had forewarning.

I stop and take a deep breath in front of the door. He's just another customer. I've worked with plenty of celebrities at past jobs. He's nothing special. He clearly doesn't remember me. So I have nothing to worry about. He'll try on the tux and be out of my life once again. Hopefully, this time for good.

He's texting on his phone when I approach and doesn't look up even as I hang the tux on the hook inside the dressing room. "Let me know if you need anything."

The curtain rattles across the rod when I yank it closed and return to the counter. I put Mrs. Roberts' blouse on a shelf under the counter and drum my fingers on the countertop. I'll finish repairing the blouse once he leaves. It certainly wouldn't look good if I damaged her blouse after agreeing to fix the half a dozen garments she brought in. I should've directed her to the couple of local women who do an excellent job mending clothes like I do for anyone else that asks about repairing clothes. But, when she told me Franny referred her to me and hesitantly explained her eyes just weren't what they used to be and she couldn't see well enough to sew anymore, I couldn't say no.

The curtain slides open, and he steps out, frowning. "I told Mitch I have my own damn tux. This is a mess. Someone screwed up the measurements. Are you sure you brought me the right one?"

I straighten my spine and run my tongue over the inside of my teeth. The tux is clearly too large in several areas.

"I assure you, it's the correct tux. I ordered it based on the measurements provided." I march over, scanning him. "I'll retake your measurements. I can make the proper adjustments. You will have to come in for a final fitting."

"This was the final fitting."

"Correct, but normally I would have taken the measurements myself. I went off the ones given as a courtesy. It is, of course, up to you. You're welcome to take the tux elsewhere for adjustments."

He scowls down. "I don't have time for this. I'll wear one of my own."

"Franny and Mitch chose this particular custom design. If you wear a standard tux, you won't match the rest of the marriage party and you'll disrupt their plans. Is that what you wish to do?"

I used to think his eyes were the exact same shade as the green stripe on my grandmother's antique chairs. But, as he glares down at me from his six-foot-three height, they're closer to the color of pond scum.

"Make it quick."

I grab the measuring tape from the small, hidden cupboard outside the dressing area and suck in a breath. He's just a customer. A rude, entitled one. I've dealt with plenty of those in the past.

The length of the pants and arms is perfect. I compare the new measurements to the ones I was given. "Have you lost weight recently?"

His gaze meets mine and darts away. "A bit."

He's probably slimming down for a new acting role or something.

"That would explain the difference."

Franny and Mitch's wedding is only a week away. I already have a full schedule. It's May and the wedding season is in full swing. If it weren't for Franny, I'd tell him to go elsewhere. She's one of the few genuine friendships I've made since moving to New Hampshire, and I don't want to disappoint her. I also owe her for the huge spike in business lately. Her and Mitch's celebrity wedding is a first for Granite Cove, and all the local businesses are seeing their sales skyrocket.

I scroll through my calendar, checking for a suitable time to schedule his fitting. Lenore will definitely handle that one. I'll go over every step with her beforehand. It should be fairly straightforward after I make the adjustments. She'll only have to bring him the tux to try on.

"I have an opening on Thursday morning at eleven o'clock. Will that work for you?" It dang well better.

He scowls as he taps on his phone. "Fine."

"You can change and leave the tux hanging up in the dressing room." I spin away.

"You'd probably get more male customers if you didn't have all these frou-frou decorations."

I slowly turn back. He's waving his hands around at the entire back of the store as he steps into the dressing room. I intentionally decorated this part of the store in a fairy-tale theme for my brides and other special occasion dress wearers. Yes, it is feminine. So are most of my clients.

Besides, it's not like it's over the top. The white-and-gold color scheme is elegant and tasteful. It's not hot pink or anything.

"Thank you so much for your unsolicited opinion. I'll be sure to redesign my store to suit your masculine comfort."

I yank the curtain closed so I don't have to see his too handsome face or the smirk spreading across it.

Chapter Two

The garden path meanders past manicured hedges and overflowing flower gardens. Rebecca would know the names of all the plants, but the rose is the only one I can identify. It probably has some fancy name, and experts would cringe if they heard me simply call it a rose. Kind of like how I cringe when a customer mixes up the types of fabric when they describe a garment they want me to make for them, and then I have to backtrack when I realize they meant something completely different.

I glance over my shoulder at the giant white house and the wedding reception happening in the yard. People dance and laugh under the massive white tent. Franny and Mitch's wedding is an amazing success. There were only a few dry eyes when Franny walked down the aisle and they said their vows. I shed a few myself.

Granted, one or two might've been because I'm feeling sorry for myself.

The path branches off in different directions, and I take the one that will take me farther away from the merriment so I can wallow a bit in silence and privacy before returning to the party.

It's not like I'm not happy for Franny. I am. If Mom hadn't pointed out I'm seven years older than Franny and still single, my loneliness probably wouldn't have crossed my mind. I should've known when she asked me how old Franny was. It's not like Mom has ever met Franny. Why would she care how old she is except to use the opportunity to once again point out I'm her only single offspring?

The path ends in an enclosed garden. A small pond with adorable red, wooden, arched bridges fills most of the area. There are cement benches around the perimeter. I sit on the closest one and stare at the lily pads with the pink-and-white flowers. Spring was certainly the right choice to have a wedding here. It's not too hot and the flowers are blooming, providing a beautiful backdrop.

A bright orange fish swims by. Then another, and then a white one with orange spots. It's a koi pond. How beautiful.

I scan the pond for different colors. There's a black spotted one, too. I follow its progress toward one of the bridges.

A blond head peers into the pond on the other side of the bridge.

So much for solitude.

It's a young boy. I search the garden for his parents. Should he be alone? How old is old enough for a kid to be unsupervised?

How old was I when I was left alone? Being the youngest of four, I was never alone. Not until I was a teenager.

He's not a teenager, but close. He is tall and rather gangly. He appears to be all elbows and knees from this angle.

He stands and walks over the bridge, staring into the pond the entire time. With his height, maybe he is a teenager. He stops about ten feet away from me and sits on the ground underneath a large tree.

"The koi fish are beautiful, aren't they? I had no idea this pond was back here. Hard to believe they're related to tiny goldfish."

He continues to stare into the pond and doesn't spare me a glance. "They're not. Koi and goldfish are entirely distinct species of fish. Koi are a type of carp, and goldfish were created from a type of carp, but they're not the same."

"Good to know."

He shrugs. "I like knowing things."

"That's a good habit to have."

He stares at me with a wrinkled frown on his face. "Some people find it annoying."

"Why would knowledge be annoying?"

A tiny smirk appears at the corner of his mouth. "That's what I think, too."

"What has your attention over there?"

"One with light blue spots. They're rarer."

"Oh yeah? I want to see." I stroll over and peer into the pond. "What other colors do they come in?"

"Orange, yellow, white, black, blue, gold. They're usually a mixture like those." He points to a group of orange-and-white ones with black spots.

"Thank you for teaching me something new today."

He shrugs.

"Are you and your family on Mitch's side or Franny's?" Probably not too subtle, but I don't feel comfortable with him being out here all alone.

"Mitch's."

"I'm a friend of Franny's."

"She seems nice. Makes awesome brownies."

I laugh. "Yes, she does. You should try her cupcakes. They're addictive."

"You got any kids?"

"Nope, just me, myself, and I." I eye the reasonably flat stone a few feet from him and sit. Hopefully, my dress won't be stained when I get up. It's not a great advertisement for my store if I saunter around in ripped or stained clothing. "How about you? Siblings? Parents?"

"No siblings. I'm not a robot, so I have the required parents, but that's not what you mean."

"Very funny. I'd like to have a robot. It could do all the cleaning I hate to do."

"I'd have it do much more interesting stuff than clean."

"Oh yeah? Like what?"

He stares up at the sky for a moment and then shrugs. "Just stuff."

"Homework?"

"Nah, I can do my own homework."

"Hmm...drive you around? You're not old enough to drive yet, are you?"

He rolls his eyes. "No, but I have a driver for that."

So he's rich.

"Can your robot fly? Oh, I know. You'd have your robot take you all over the world or into space. That would be amazing."

He laughs. "Yeah, that would be kind of cool. The space part."

"You want to walk back to the wedding together and find your parents?"

He frowns and shakes his head.

"They're probably worried about you. Do they know where you are?"

"He thinks I'm with Amy. Besides, I have my phone. I can always text him if I need him."

Him...so a father, not a mother. "Who's Amy?"

Another eye roll. "My nanny."

Thinks he's too old for one, probably. "Dare I ask where she is?"

"Last time I saw her, she was downing champagne and giggling."

Oh boy. Perhaps his nanny is enjoying the festivities a little too much.

I nibble on my bottom lip. I can't just leave him alone here. I guess there's no one who will really miss me. Franny is obviously busy. Rebecca is a bridesmaid, so she's busy, too. She asked me to keep an eye on her brother, Drew, but he's with Ian and he was playing with Olivia's twins earlier.

I look sideways at the boy. "How old are you?"

"Why?"

"Because my friends have boys that might be around your age, and I thought you might like to meet them."

He stares at me silently. Is he considering it?

"I'm twelve."

"The twins are ten or eleven, and Drew is a little older."

"Are they nice?"

My heart clenches. "They are. I'll come with you."

"Will you stay?"

"Of course." I'm not going to leave this kid alone. "You going to tell me your name?"

He gives me a small smile. "Trevor."

"It's nice to meet you, Trevor. My name is Kelly."

He follows me back through the gardens. I hear boys' laughter and head in that direction. Trevor's steps slow as we get closer.

"Timmy and Tommy are the twins. Their mom, Olivia, is one of Franny's bridesmaids. Drew is Rebecca's brother. She's one of the bridesmaids, too."

We step into a clearing with a low maze of hedges. The bushes are only waist high. The boys, along with Luke and Ian, are playing a tag hide and seek.

Drew spots us and jogs over. He stops in front of us and waves at Trevor. "Hi. Do you want to play?"

I smile. Drew always has a smile on his face whenever I see him. His friendliness is contagious and uplifting.

"Drew, this is Trevor."

"Come on." Drew runs back to the maze.

Trevor glances at me and then shrugs.

"I'll wait right here. Unfortunately, this dress wasn't made to play hide and seek in."

He strolls over with his hands in his pockets. Drew introduces him to everyone, and they fill him in on the rules and start a new game.

A smile appears on Trevor's face within a few minutes. By the end of the first round, he's grinning and laughing with them.

I sit on a wooden bench in front of a tall hedge and under a giant tree. I can monitor him from here and he can see me. I promised him I would stay.

He texts something on his phone a few times, but other than glancing in my direction, his entire focus is on the game. Lights flicker on as dusk descends. They're strung in the trees and placed around the maze.

Olivia arrives and she and Luke sit on a bench in the corner. Rebecca watches from a distance. I stand to join her until I see Ian heading in her direction. I sit back down.

"Thank you for watching over my son."

I gape up at Holden Fox. He stands next to me in his tux, which fits him like a glove—thank you very much.

I snap my mouth closed and look at Trevor. "Trevor is your son?"

"You didn't know?"

"No, I only knew he was a kid by himself."

He scowls. "Yeah, I fired his nanny. She's drunk and barely conscious. Came with excellent references, but I guess you never know. Trev texted me Franny's friend, Kelly, was keeping him company and introducing him to other boys to play with." He smirks. "Franny said you're her only friend named Kelly, so it must be you. She assured me you are trustworthy and not going to abscond with my son."

"Was that a concern?" Wait, of course, he's a celebrity. He probably does have to worry about abduction more than the average parent.

He runs his hand through his hair. "I have to consider a lot of things as a parent I never thought I would."

His hair is much lighter than Trevor's, but I suppose he has highlights or something. Or Trevor could take after his mother. Who is his mother? I've carefully avoided reading or watching anything that mentions Holden Fox over the years. I didn't even know he had a son. Or that he was married.

"Listen, I'll pay you for your time." He takes out his wallet and flips through a stack of bills.

You have got to be kidding me.

I stand. "I don't want your money, Mr. Fox."

He searches my face like he can't believe I'm serious.

"I'll just say goodbye to Trevor, if you don't mind."

I don't wait for him to answer. I wave at Trevor as I get close. "I have to get going, Trevor. I wanted to say goodbye."

He jogs closer and frowns. "You're leaving?"

"Yes, it's been a long day. Your dad's here." I jerk my thumb over my shoulder without turning around.

He waves at his dad. "Am I going to see you again?"

"Well, I own a dress shop in town. It's called Dress to Impress. So, if you're ever back in Granite Cove, you can drop in and say hello."

"Okay, I guess."

He seems disappointed. I bite my lip. Why did Holden Fox have to be his father? "Can I give you a hug?"

He wraps his arms around me and I give him a squeeze. His head is almost even with mine. He'll tower over me in another year or so.

"Never stop learning, Trevor."

He pulls away and gives me half a smile. I clear my suddenly constricted throat. Dang, this kid is really getting to me.

I wave at Rebecca, Ian, Olivia, and Luke as I stride past.

Maybe my mother is right and my biological clock is not only ticking, but it's releasing kid-wanting hormones throughout my body.

God, wouldn't that just be my luck! It's not bad enough my mother feels it's her mission on earth to pressure me to marry and produce children? Now my own body is starting its own campaign?

Chapter Three

Navigating the village sidewalks during the summer can be like battling an ocean current. The swarms of people resemble the crowds I grew accustomed to when I lived in Manhattan, not the sweet little lakeside town of Granite Cove.

I duck into an alleyway, lean against the cool brick wall, and take a long sip of my iced coffee. Franny's coffee is the best. I don't know what she does to make it taste so good, but it really hits the spot. It would've tasted even better with the salted caramel cupcake I originally walked to The Sweet Spot for, but they sold out of my favorite treat.

According to Sally's whispered explanation, Holden Fox snagged the last one. I'm not sure why she bothered whispering. It's not like it's a big secret he's been renting a place on the lake for the past couple of weeks. He's probably hiding out after the huge custody battle over Trevor that's been splashed all over the tabloids and internet all summer.

Poor kid. My heart broke for him when I read the news. I wonder if I'll get a chance to see him again while he's here—at least I assume he's here. Holden won full custody, so Trevor should be here, too, right? Unless he shipped him off somewhere with a new nanny.

Even here in the shade, the August heat is oppressive. I place the sweating plastic cup against the side of my neck for a moment. I need to get back to the shop. Thankfully, it's only a few blocks up the street.

I take a long swallow of coffee and shove off the wall. Time to slip back into the throngs of tourists. I shouldn't complain. My bottom line certainly loves the summer surge of shoppers.

I clutch my coffee close to my chest so no one bumps into it and sidestep the shorts-and-tank-top-clad teenagers occupying most of the sidewalk. I peek into Blossoms as I pass to see if Rebecca is busy. I could use a few minutes of conversation. She's behind the counter, but there's a line of customers. Conversation with her will have to wait until book club next week.

Luke's latest release kept me up way past my bedtime over the weekend. When Olivia selected her fiancé's book for book club, I was nervous I wouldn't like it and not know what to say when it came time to discuss the book. Thrillers aren't normally my thing, but I couldn't put it down. I wonder if Luke will be at book club to discuss his book.

The café door opens abruptly, and a man barrels into me. My coffee drenches my chest. The ice-cold liquid trickles down my cleavage. I hunch my shoulders and stare at my stained blouse. *Bollocks!*

"Sorry."

The husky drawl snaps my head up.

Holden Fox.

Of course it is. He's become the bane of my existence lately. The universe must really hate me.

He stares at my soaked chest and winces. "Um…I'll pay for that, of course."

I narrow my eyes. "Dang straight, you will."

"Relax. I said I would." He strides over to a truck parked illegally in a no-parking zone and places his packages on the passenger seat.

"Relax? Did you seriously just tell me to relax?" I chuck my cup into the trash can, march over to his truck, and plant my fists on my hips. "What is your problem?"

"My problem is you and your rude, insufferable, entitled behavior!" I point to the no-parking sign clearly displayed in front of his truck. "This is a no-parking zone."

He folds his arms over his chest. "I was in the restaurant for a minute. Stop blowing things out of proportion."

"And what if there was a fire or something? It's for emergency vehicles. You can park in a parking spot like the rest of us mortals."

"If you're so worried about me blocking an emergency, then why don't you stop haranguing me and let me leave?"

"You are unbelievable!"

He takes two steps closer to me. "And you are an uptight harridan."

My mouth drops open. Did he just call me an uptight, bossy, *old* woman?

"First, you insult my store and my competence. Next, you try to pay me for spending time with Trevor. Then you steal the last caramel cupcake, waste my coffee, and ruin my blouse. Now, you dare call me uptight, bossy, and old?"

I poke him in the chest. "You are an asshole!"

I stalk down the sidewalk to my store and storm inside. Lenore looks up from the cash register where she's ringing up a customer. She stares at me and then my blouse. Her eyes grow wide.

"Um...everything okay?"

"Just peachy. I'll be in the back if you need me."

Luckily, I own a dress shop. I snag a new blouse off the rack of clothes and snip off the tags. You better believe I'm going to bill mister famous celebrity for the new blouse and cleaning of this one.

I peel off the wet, sticky blouse and grimace at my bra. It's soaked through, too. I close my eyes and picture a beach with palm trees. There's a gentle, cooling breeze and a hammock strung between two trees. I'm reclining in the hammock listening to the waves lap at the shore and have a cocktail in my hand. There's even an umbrella sticking out of the glass.

I sigh and open my eyes. I need a vacation.

The bra gets tossed on top of the stained blouse and I search through the intimates rack for my bra size. It's a darn good thing I have to carry them for the specialty dresses. Perhaps it's time I create a dedicated section for intimates out on the floor of the shop. I always keep them back here and wait for a customer to request them or I suggest them if a dress needs a particular undergarment. It's not like there are any other options for customers located close by. They have to go to the mall.

Once dressed, I plop down at my desk and drop my head to the surface. Did I really just screech at Holden Fox in the middle of town?

Ugh, I suppose it's way too much to hope no one witnessed my meltdown.

I'll just hide back here for the rest of the day, or maybe week.

By the time Lenore pokes her head in a little while later, I managed to drag myself upright.

"Anything I can do for you, boss?"

"Not unless you can teleport me to Bora Bora for an all-expenses-paid trip."

She chuckles. "If I could do that, I'd transport us both. Wouldn't that be something?"

"It sure would."

She tilts her head to the side. "Anything you want to talk about?"

I stare at her earnest round face and shake my head. Her heart is in the right place, but I doubt Lenore has ever had a thought that didn't also pass her lips. She's not one for keeping secrets. The last thing I need is my personal business broadcast all over town.

"Thanks, Lenore, but it's just one of those days."

"Okay. I'll be out front if you change your mind."

I drum up a smile for her and flip up the top of my laptop. I might as well get some work done while I hide out back here.

* * *

"Delivery."

A giant bouquet of flowers with legs and high heels fills the doorway to the backroom.

Rebecca cants her head around the display and grins. "Where do you want them?"

"Those are for me?" Who would send me flowers? The last time I got flowers delivered they were from my aunt for my thirtieth birthday a couple years ago.

"They sure are." She struts across to my desk and I scramble to clear a spot. "They come with a message, too."

The floral scents emanating from the bouquet remind me of spring.

She sets down the vase and plucks a small blue envelope from somewhere in the top of the flowers. I reach out to take it, but she holds it out of my range between her two fingers.

"You've been holding out on me." Her bright red lips are pursed. The white sleeveless dress she purchased from my shop flows over her cocked hip.

"I have?" I frown at the flowers. "I don't think so."

She hands over the card.

I flip open the envelope and read the silver card inside with her logo on top. There's only one word on the card. *Sorry.*

"He didn't leave a name, but I recognized the western drawl. Since when do you hang out with Holden Fox and what's he sorry for?"

"My timing is perfect." Olivia walks in with a large pink-and-black box from The Sweet Spot. "I'd love to hear this story, too." She plops down the box and takes a card out of the pocket of her periwinkle blue, floral sundress. "He didn't apologize on this one."

I glance at the card. *I didn't steal it, I bought it.*

Olivia opens the box. There are a dozen caramel cupcakes inside. "He called the bakery and cajoled Franny into making them. She's ordered me not to come back unless I have all the details from you. So what is going on between you and Holden Fox? And what did you accuse him of stealing?"

Rebecca sits on the corner of my desk and plucks a cupcake out of the box. "May I?"

"By all means." I pick one up and inhale the sugary goodness from the frosting. "God, I need this." The moist, white cake melts in my mouth. The sweet caramel frosting with additional caramel drizzled on top and a sprinkle of salt supplies a nice zing to my tastebuds. "Perfection."

Olivia chuckles and selects one for herself.

Rebecca points her cupcake at me. "Start talking."

I peek at Olivia. "These are my favorite. I come in at least once a week for one—sometimes twice if it's a rough week or I decide to reward myself."

She nods and takes a bite of her cupcake.

"I went in this morning and they were all gone. Sally told me he purchased the last one."

Rebecca gazes at the flowers and the cupcakes. "All this because he bought the last cupcake?"

"Not exactly." I tell them about the coffee and our showdown on the sidewalk.

Olivia licks the frosting off her thumb and frowns. "I've only met Holden a couple of times. For the wedding and then a playdate with his son and the boys, but that doesn't sound like the same man. He was so nice when we talked." She glances at Rebecca. "Right?"

"He was, but obviously Kelly has experienced a different side to him than we have." She gestures to the flowers and cupcakes again. "Though at least he seems to recognize the errors of his ways and is man enough to apologize. We have to give him points for that. Unless you don't want us to. Say the word and we'll hate him forever."

Olivia nods. "Absolutely."

I laugh and lean back in my chair. "Thanks, but I'm not usually one to hold a grudge. He's still not one of my favorite people, but I'm willing to let bygones be bygones. He can't be all bad since Trevor is pretty terrific."

Olivia dusts off her hands. "That he is. Timmy and Tommy think he's super cool ever since he taught them how to whistle."

Rebecca crosses her legs. "He and Drew bonded over cars. Trevor was a fount of information."

"Yeah, he's great. His dad, not so much."

Olivia sighs heavily. "Franny is going to be so disappointed. She thought for sure a romance was brewing between the two of you."

"Tell her I'm sorry to disappoint her, but it's not going to happen."

Chapter Four

A familiar sandy-haired boy strolls into the store dressed in shorts and a T-shirt. He stops and scans the entire store as if he's cataloging every inch and filing it away. My lips twitch. It's been a few months, but I swear he's grown a few inches.

"It's about time you came to say hello." I saunter out from behind the counter.

Trevor grins when he spots me. "Hi."

I give him a one-armed hug, and he rests his head against my shoulder. I glance out the front window of the store. "Did you give another nanny the slip?"

"Naw, Dad finally agreed not to hire anymore. When he can't be with me, Gram or Grandpa are."

Trevor wanders to the back of the store. "You really must like fairy tales or princesses or something, huh?"

I chuckle as I follow him. "I do, and since I cater to brides and other special occasion dressy attire for women, it seems to work. Not too many men shop here. I only get the occasional grooms and such for tuxes."

"Did you know they named the tuxedo after a park? Some designer copied the style from a prince or something."

"I didn't know. I guess I never really thought about it. Interesting, though. Did you read that somewhere?"

He shrugs and stuffs his hands into the front pockets of his shorts. "Yeah, it was in an article. I was bored and had nothing else to read."

"Do your grandparents know where you are?" I'd hate to think they're worrying about him.

He gives me a sideways glance. "You mean here in New Hampshire?"

"No, I mean in town. Here, with me? I would hope they're aware you're in New Hampshire. Didn't you say they're watching you?"

"I said they watch me when Dad can't. Usually it's in Texas on their ranch."

"Oh." I glance behind me. Does that mean Holden is here in town?

Trevor gazes toward the front of the store. "He's waiting in the truck. I think he's afraid of you. Said you yelled at him over cupcakes or something."

I wince. "Let me give you some sage advice." I put my arm around his shoulder. "Never get between a woman and her sweets fix, especially when she's having a bad day."

He smirks.

"I'm not kidding. This is prime information you'll be thankful for some day."

"Okay. Why were you having a bad day?"

I wave my hand in front of me. "Oh, well, that is a long story. And not a topic I care to waste my time with you rehashing. What have you been up to this summer? Do you like it here in Granite Cove?"

"Yeah, it's pretty cool. The lake is nice. Dad's been teaching me to fish. A boat came with the cabin rental. I went tubing for the first time."

"What's that?"

"You sit in a tube being pulled behind the boat."

"Oh, that sounds like fun. You wore a life vest, right?"

"Yeah, Dad always makes me wear one in the boat."

"Good. I've never been tubing or waterskiing. I've been in a boat before, but we never did any water sports when I was a kid. One of my brothers did some sailing if I remember right, but that's about it."

"How many brothers do you have?"

"Three, all older."

"That must've been pretty cool growing up."

I shrug. "Depends on how you look at it, I suppose. They're bossy and have always treated me like a baby. It gets kind of old."

That was probably too negative. "It has its good points, too." I just can't think of any at the moment.

He stares at me.

Crap, now I have to elaborate. I can't tell him they picked on me all the time and still do. "It was never too hard to get a ride from one of them when I needed to go somewhere." He doesn't need to know I preferred public transportation than enduring their endless teasing.

"Do they live around here?"

"No, they're all back in Chicago. That's where I grew up."

"I've been to Chicago. They have some good museums."

Trevor is the only twelve-year-old boy I know who would comment on the quality of a city's museums. "Yes, they do."

"You close soon, don't you?"

I glance at my watch. A little less than an hour to go. "Yes, at six."

"You want to have dinner with me?"

"Sure, if it's okay with your dad." I doubt Holden wants to sit around that long in his truck. But he could have errands to run or something. What do I know?

"He doesn't mind."

"Okay, we can walk over to the docks and eat at Billing's Creamery. Have you eaten there yet?"

"We got ice cream there a couple of times. But I thought we could eat at the cabin instead. I had Dad buy those cupcakes you like from Franny's bakery."

"Oh."

Does that mean Holden would join us? Dinner with Holden Fox? Not on my list of favorite things to do. In fact, it might be on my list of things to avoid at all costs.

Trevor stares at me patiently.

I can't very well tell him I have other plans when I just said we could eat at Billings.

His shoulders slump and his gaze drops to the floor. "Dad said you'd say no."

Thinks he knows me, does he? He was probably counting on me saying no. Didn't want to tell his son not to invite me so he wouldn't be the bad guy. He set me up to be the one to say no instead. Major miscalculation on his part. There's no way I'm disappointing Trevor.

"That sounds great. I'll need directions, and tell me what I can bring."

He grins and pulls out his phone. "I'll AirDrop the directions to you. You don't have to bring anything. We already got everything."

My phone beeps, and I pull it out of my pocket.

"Six-thirty good?" Trevor is already halfway to the door.

"Um, yeah." I accept the directions and glance up. The door closes behind him. I guess it's settled then.

I huff out a breath and pace over to the counter. How the hell did I get roped into having dinner with Holden Fox?

Oh yeah, I really like his kid and didn't want to disappoint him.

This evening will not be awkward at all. I bend over on the counter, resting my forehead against the cool surface.

He's just a man. An insufferable, conceited man who happens to be a celebrity listed as one of the most beautiful people in the world—more than once. A man who doesn't remember me.

I snap my head up.

Why am I dwelling on something so insignificant he doesn't even remember it? He apologized for his recent, atrocious behavior. I can be the better person and rise above. I will attend this dinner for Trevor's sake. Maybe I'll get lucky and Holden will make an excuse and not attend.

* * *

The signs warning this is a private road switch to private property. I glance over at my phone and the GPS again. According to Trevor's directions, this is the right road. If you can call this dirt track into the woods a road.

Towering evergreens loom over my car on either side. If the cabin they're renting is on the lake, shouldn't I see the lake? I could swear I turned away from the lake a few miles back.

My car crests a small rise. I step on the brake and gasp. Well, there's the lake. It's spread out in front of me for miles. What a view!

The road dips and turns. A dark green cabin perches on the shore of the lake. The front door opens, and Trevor steps out waving. I smile and return his wave while I park next to Holden's truck.

When he said he'd rented a cabin, I thought it might be a celebrity euphemism for one of the many multimillion-dollar mansions lining the lake. But this is really a modest cabin.

Trevor opens my door as I shut off the engine. "You made it."

"I did. I was a little nervous I was in the wrong place on that road."

Trevor frowns and glances at the road. "I guess I should've warned you."

"That's all right. I guess I'm still a city girl in certain ways."

"Come on. Dad's already got the grill going. We're having steak." He stops and whirls around. "You're not a vegetarian, are you?"

"No, I like steak just fine."

"There are many health benefits to becoming a vegetarian, but I couldn't do that to Grandpa. It's like an unwritten law or something to a Texas ranch owner that you have to be a carnivore. More specifically, an omnivore."

"I can see how that might be an issue." I follow him into the house and stop. The entire visible back wall of the cabin is glass. If it wasn't for the deck off the back of the house, it would appear as if the house floated on top of the lake. A dock with a boat attached to it is just beyond the deck.

The floor plan is open with the kitchen and living room sharing the space. Trevor opens a slider, which disappears into the wall, and glances back at me. Holden stands in front of a grill to the right when I step onto the deck. His gaze wanders over me, and he gives me a slight nod.

Not exactly a friendly welcome. "Good evening. Thank you for inviting me."

His brow quirks and he glances at Trevor. Okay, that came out a bit more formal than I planned. It's not a ballroom. It's just dinner at a cabin on the lake. I've got this.

"What can I do to help?"

Trevor points to a picnic table laden with food and place settings for three. So much for my hope Holden would disappear.

"It's all set." He sits down on the side with two place settings and taps the bench next to him. "Have a seat."

I really should have changed out of my skirt and blouse after work into something more casual. I sit and then swing my legs over.

Trevor hops up. "Oh, what would you like to drink?" He opens the lid of a cooler filled with bottles and cans. "There's soda, water, and beer. Dad said you might prefer wine. We've got that in the house. Would you like red or white?"

I smile. "Water is fine, thanks." How many twelve-year-olds would know about wine and offer a choice between red or white? I certainly wouldn't have.

Trevor sits and points to the various containers. "There's potato salad, pasta salad, regular salad."

Holden turns from the grill. "Rare or medium rare?"

I'm tempted to say well-done just to be difficult. "Medium rare, please."

No one speaks as he brings over the steaks and we fill our plates.

The hum from boat motors on the lake is the only sound to break the silence besides the occasional utensil scraping a plate.

"It's delicious. Thank you again for having me." I briefly glance at Holden before smiling at Trevor.

"We can go for a boat ride after dinner if you like."

Prolong the torture of Holden clearly not wanting me here? Um, no, thank you. I bite my lip as I stare at Trevor's eager face.

"How about we save that for another time? Are there any games you and I can play?"

"Do you like chess?"

Not my best. "I know the basics, but I admit I'm not that good. You'll probably trounce me within minutes."

"There's charades. Trev, you always enjoy playing, right?"

Trevor nods and looks at me. "Do you like charades?"

"I don't think I've ever played. That's where you have to get someone to guess a word by acting it out?" I bet it's one of Holden's favorite games, but is it really one of Trevor's?

"You've never played charades?" Trevor frowns tightly with his eyebrows pinched together.

I can't be the only person who's never played charades. "My family didn't play games when I was a kid."

"It's fairly straightforward. You already said the basic rules. Trev, why don't you go get the cards while I clean up?"

Trevor jumps up and goes inside. I swing my legs over the bench and stack the plates together. Holden puts away the containers of salads while I bring in the rest of the dishes. He turns and folds his arms over his chest.

"Thanks for coming, for Trevor's sake. He really took to you at the wedding and has been asking to see you again."

"Of course, he's a great kid." Don't worry, Mr. Celebrity, I'm well aware the invitation is from Trevor and not you. I wouldn't have accepted otherwise.

"Yeah, he is."

The weight of his stare as I rinse the dishes and load the dishwasher makes heat bloom across the back of my neck. I shut the door and face him. "Something else you want to say?"

Trevor rounds the corner with a small box in his hand. "Found them."

"We'll play outside." Holden jerks his head toward the deck, and Trevor goes outside to the picnic table.

"Just to be clear, this is a onetime thing. Our lease is up in a couple of weeks anyway, but I don't want you getting the wrong idea."

Ice forms in my veins. "You've made your point, Mr. Fox. You won't be hearing from me."

Chapter Five

"I went to this party last week, and you wouldn't believe all the hot guys dating trolls. Seriously, why am I still single? I'm a solid ten on anyone's scale." Suzanne rolls her eyes and rests her arm on the back of the couch. "I'm sure money or ambition had to play into some of the matchups. What other reasons could there be?"

I catch myself in time to stop the eye roll her comment is begging for. Her and Candace are both bottle blondes. Their natural color is closer to my own brunette. They both have blue eyes. Although I know for a fact, Candace wears colored contacts. I doubt either of them has enough fat to register on one of those fat-measuring calipers which one of my roommates used to carry around in her purse.

She is attractive. A slew of professionals and a couple of surgeries have ensured she's a woman that turns guys' heads. I would never describe her as a solid ten, however. Of course, my less-than-stellar opinion of her personality or intelligence may be influencing my judgment. She's always treated me like some stray even though I'm the blood relation and she's only here because her sister married one of my brothers.

"The guys could be mature enough or intelligent enough to know a beautiful personality is more rewarding than appearance. Beauty is subjective and fleeting."

Suzanne stares at me like I spoke a different language and then turns back to her sister and widens her eyes dramatically as if to say, "Who is this idiot and why is she talking?" Candace's lips twist repeatedly like she's desperately trying not to laugh. She rests her hand over her sister's and glances at me and back to Suzanne.

"Kelly is what we affectionately call terminally single."

Why the heck did I come home for Thanksgiving?

My sister-in-law smirks and chuckles. "I told Thomas he should set you up with the new doctor at the hospital, but he said it would be a waste of time."

"Doctor? What's his portfolio look like?"

Could Suzanne be any more shallow? Is how much money a guy has really her number-one requirement?

"He's not for you." Candace slices her gaze toward me and back to her sister. "I'll explain later."

I'm sitting right here. Does she really believe I'm too blind or dumb to catch her meaning? The doctor is good enough for me, but not her sister. He's probably thrice divorced and old enough to be my grandfather. She's tried to set me up with similar men before. I'd thank Thomas for intervening, but his comment probably reflected on a less-than-flattering opinion of me rather than the doctor. My brothers have joked about my poor taste in men for years.

Granted, they're not entirely unwarranted. It's not surprising I tend to go for the complete opposite of the men in my family. No professionals. Unemployed? Even better. No polished gentlemen from an upper-middle-class family. Broken home? School dropout? Bad-boy reputation? Ding ding ding.

I sound like a textbook psychological example of a rebellious teenager. Except I'm thirty-two years old and so tired of playing the role of the black sheep in the family. The one who never quite fits in. I'm the proverbial square peg trying to fit into a round hole.

My brothers all stand with my father by the glass bar cart—as they do at every family gathering before and after the meal. They all have the same brown hair and cleft chins. Even their receding hairlines match. Their gray or white dress shirts and black pants probably all come from the same store.

Brian's wife, Madison, excused herself some time ago to check on her newborn son. Thomas and Candace's nanny could probably use the help since she's watching all my nieces and nephews in a room upstairs. I hope they're paying her well. There are six of them, after all, two for each of my brothers. Brian and Madison's nanny quit recently, and apparently it's been quite the upheaval since Madison's maternity leave ends soon. James and Caroline generously gave their nanny the day off. They probably didn't anticipate Caroline would be called back to the hospital for an emergency surgery.

As a kid, I resented being separated from the rest of the family. Kids were never allowed at formal meals or parties. Now, I envy the kids. They're probably playing games and having fun.

How often are my brothers and their wives alone with their children? That's probably a nasty thought on my part. It's not like I have anything against having a nanny. Caroline and Madison both work. Candace doesn't, but apparently her social obligations are too much for her to manage and raise her children without help. Nasty thought number two. Okay, I may have been here a day too long. Whenever I come back for a visit, my kindness and understanding seem to take a leave of absence and it's all I can do to stop myself from sniping at my family.

I grip the gray cushion of the couch between my fists and stare at my royal blue pumps against the white-and-gray rug. My mother redecorated the living room last year, and everything in the room is either a shade of gray, white, or glass. My shoes and the matching dress are the brightest colors in the entire room. Suzanne and Candace both wear white. My mother and grandmother are both garbed in black.

They've been whispering in the corner for a good half hour now. It's typical behavior for them, and they could be discussing anything from a new color scheme, family gossip, or they could be cooking up some awful plan to see me married and pregnant by the end of the year. It wouldn't be the first time.

They've been trying to marry me off for over a decade. They'd probably arrange a marriage for me if they could. Both of them are strong feminists, so why do they still insist on seeing me married and bearing children? It's like I have little value otherwise.

Not that I wouldn't like to have both someday. But it will definitely be with a man of my choosing, not my family's.

Brenda appears in the doorway and signals my mother the meal is ready. My parents' housekeeper must be at least in her sixties. What will my parents do when she retires?

"Dinner is ready. Let's go in, shall we?" Mom makes her way to the dining room, and we all trail behind her.

The silver has been brought out and polished. The table shines beneath the crystal chandelier. A crisp white tablecloth. Mother's white china with a silver border. Crystal wine glasses. It's all very elegant. So why do I feel the urge to splash around some of the red wine from the glasses and add some color?

I can imagine all their horrified stares and gasps directed my way.

My grandmother clears her throat. When she has my attention, she tilts her head to the chair next to her. Not a strand of her snow-white hair moves. She must go through bottles of hairspray every week.

The rest of the family has already taken their seats. Even Madison has made a reappearance and sits next to Brian. I slide into the chair next to my grandmother. There's an empty chair next to me waiting if Caroline returns. She's not likely to provide much of a reprieve from whatever my grandmother has planned for me. Caroline usually talks medical jargon with my brothers and father.

"How are you, Grand-Mère?" I place my napkin across my lap and smile in her direction. As far as I know, we're not French, but she's insisted on being called the French version of grandmother my entire life. I once asked my mother why and was told to stop asking silly questions.

"I'm not getting any younger, and neither are you." She waves her finger next to my face, and a waft of her heavy perfume tickles my nose.

"That's generally the way it works."

"Don't be impertinent. When are you going to stop gallivanting around the world and move back to Chicago where you belong?"

"I'm hardly gallivanting anymore. I live in Granite Cove, New Hampshire. It's a lovely town. You should come for a visit."

"What on earth for?"

"To visit me and see where I live. See my dress shop." The chances of that happening are somewhat less than an apocalyptic event occurring right now to save me from this conversation.

"I see no reason to traipse around the woods. It's time for you to move home."

"Granite Cove may be a small town, but we do have roofs over our heads and even indoor plumbing."

"Always with the sarcasm. In my day, children respected their elders."

Right. Bite my tongue and endure. What was I thinking to speak my mind?

"I'm sorry, Grand-Mère."

James passes the bread bowl to me. I lift the napkin and take a roll.

My grandmother slaps my hand and stuffs the roll back in the basket. "You can eat bread after you find a husband."

She passes the bread bowl to my mother on her left, who passes it on to Brian without taking a roll.

If I snatch the bowl back from Brian and chomp into a roll, both my mother and grandmother are likely to have apoplectic fits. The rest of my family will only roll their eyes at my latest transgression.

Nope, I will not be the subject of another family dinner if I can help it. Besides, it's not worth the defiance. Grand-Mère is not going to change now.

It's a miracle I don't have an eating disorder. One minute I'm told to stop eating something or I'll get fat, and then a few minutes later my mother will tell me I'm not eating enough. I grab a slab of turkey and dump it on my plate. Any hunger I might've had evaporated, but I'll have to swallow a few bites to avoid any further comments.

As soon as dinner is over, I'm changing my flight to tomorrow. What the hell was I thinking staying through the weekend?

Oh yes, I was feeling lonely and thinking spending time with my family might help.

It's funny how time and distance can paint a rosier glow and blur the memories. Then reality smacks you in the face and reminds you just why you took off after high school and moved across the country.

My mother monopolizes my grandmother's attention throughout the rest of the meal. Mom has always had the ability to know when I'm about to explode. She glances at me repeatedly like I'm a ticking time bomb.

Storm out of a few holiday dinners and you get a bad reputation.

The few pieces of turkey and asparagus I ate roll around my stomach like a circus act. The two glasses of wine I consumed have encased me in an overly bright, warm glow. I've never had a high tolerance for alcohol, and drinking on an empty stomach probably wasn't the best idea I've had.

I slip into the bathroom after dinner while everyone else returns to the living room. I scroll my phone searching for a flight home tomorrow instead of Sunday. Two layovers means I'll spend the day in airports, but it beats more family time—aka the judgment zone.

My steps are a little lighter as I enter the living room. My mother is likely to see right through any excuse I come up with, but my sanity is more important right now.

Suzanne gasps as I walk in the room.

Crap! Do I have toilet paper stuck to my shoe? Is my dress tucked into my panties?

I do a quick scan. Nope, everything is in place.

She shows Candace and Madison her phone. "Holden Fox is cheating on his wife! There are pictures of him and some brunette at a cabin on a lake."

Why is this shocking news? And how can it be called cheating if he's divorced? And why can't I get through one single day lately without someone bringing up his name?

"You know, I met his wife once. She's even beautiful in person. You know how photos and television can make almost anyone look good. I've met celebrities in real life and been so disappointed. She must be devastated." Suzanne shakes her head, but there's still a grin etched on her face as she scrolls on her phone.

Candace leans closer. "Who's the woman?"

"It doesn't say. The picture is unclear. She's tall. Probably a model. I'm sure we'll find out soon. He can't keep her identity secret for long."

I sway closer to the group. It's a good thing he's no longer in Granite Cove. Wherever he is now will be invaded with people trying to find out who Holden's mystery woman is.

I almost feel sorry for the poor woman.

Madison peeks at Suzanne's phone. "She might just be a casual acquaintance. You can't believe everything you see on social media."

Suzanne points to her screen. "Look how close they're standing. That's not a casual acquaintance. Besides, they have to fact-check this stuff."

Candice folds her arms over her waist. "Some women have no morals. How dare she go after a married man?"

Suzanne shrugs. "Obviously, he couldn't have been happily married, or the woman wouldn't have been able to lure him away. Just because you put a ring on it doesn't mean he's off the market."

Madison rears back. Candace frowns at her sister. Suzanne enlarges the picture on the screen.

"I bet it's an actress in his latest film." She peers at her phone.

Why am I standing here listening to this? I couldn't care less who Holden Fox dates.

I glance down at her phone as I turn away. I take two steps and halt.

That cabin is the one he rented in Granite Cove.

That alleged model or actress with no morals is wearing the same exact outfit I wore when Trevor invited me over to dinner.

Oh my God! The brunette in the picture is me.

They must have taken it when he was warning me away from Trevor. That's the only time we stood close.

So much for the saying a picture is worth a thousand words. That picture got it all wrong.

I glance up and find Suzanne's gaze on me. She stares at me and then back down to her phone. "Impossible."

"What's impossible?" Candace peeks over her sister's shoulder.

Suzanne waves her hand in the air. "Nothing. I just had the most ridiculous thought. For a moment, I thought the woman in the photo bore a resemblance to Kelly." She laughs and rolls her eyes.

Candace glances back and forth between me and the picture. "Wasn't it rumored he was visiting Mitch Atwater, who lives in New Hampshire?"

Say something. Get them off track before they connect the dots.

"So?" Suzanne frowns at her sister.

Candace taps a long, red fingernail against her lips. "Didn't you mention meeting Mitch Atwater, Kelly? You sold his wife her dress, didn't you?"

A weak moment coming back to bite me in the ass. I bragged celebrities shopped at my store. Like that would make Dress to Impress more important in their eyes.

I stare at Madison and then glance at Candace and Suzanne. All three of them are staring at me open mouthed like they can't conceive of the possibility I might be the woman with Holden.

They're waiting for me to deny it.

It'd be so simple. I just have to laugh it off. They'll believe it easily. After all, it's as ridiculous as Suzanne said it is for me to be involved with Holden Fox.

"It's me."

Chapter Six

The woman's bracelet has bells which jingle every time she picks up one of the items from the conveyor belt and scans the barcode. There's a Rudolph-antlers headband stuck in her brown, curly hair. Christmas decorations already? Thanksgiving was only two days ago. I suppose that means I'll have to drag out the decorations for the store this week.

"Can you believe Holden Fox is right here in Granite Cove? We're turning into a celebrity hang out." The woman stops scanning my groceries. "I used to act in the school plays. Several people told me I had a gift."

I smile and nod. Why didn't I go to the self-checkout lane?

It was bad enough explaining the innocence of the picture to my family. I do not need the entire town knowing I'm the mystery woman splashed all over the tabloids.

Suzanne, Candace, and Madison quickly accepted the explanation I gave them about being there on an errand for Franny. I didn't see the point in telling them about Trevor or how insufferable Holden Fox really is. As far as they know, I met him one time for a brief moment. What possessed me to confess it was me in the first place?

My impulsivity rearing its ugly head again.

I grab my bags and head for the door. I spent most of yesterday on planes. At least Waldo was happy to see me and I saved some money picking him up early from the kennel. Unfortunately, I had no groceries or Thanksgiving leftovers to get me through the weekend. I should've had groceries delivered so I could hide out at home all weekend until the next big story breaks and everyone forgets all about the mystery woman with Holden Fox.

Oh well, luckily, I'm still a mystery to most of the population and I can still hide out for the weekend. My store is covered since I wasn't supposed to be home. I fully intend to take advantage of the situation.

Waldo sits patiently while I unpack the groceries at home. His large head is even with my waist and he tilts it from side to side. "Don't worry. You know I would never forget to get something for you." I unpack his treats and give him one when he gives me a paw to shake.

Someone knocks on my door. Who could that be? No one knows I'm home. One of the neighbors might've seen me. One of the downsides of living in an apartment is neighbors know when you're home. Tom and Alice are the only ones who ever knock on my door, though. They probably want to borrow milk for coffee. It's been a recurring theme since I moved in. At least they vary which neighbor they ask so it's not always me.

I grab the carton of milk and open the door. Tom usually just brings his coffee over rather than have me pour milk in a glass. I swear they must have an entire set of my glasses by now.

Rebecca stands at the door with her hand raised to knock again. She flips her dark sunglasses up and grins as she holds up her phone. "Tell me this isn't you, Miss Can't Stand Holden Fox."

Bollocks!

I step back, and she breezes past me in a black wool coat cinched at the waist. So much for nobody recognizing me.

"How did you know I was home?"

"Olivia spotted you driving in town. She told Franny. Lucinda happened to be at the bakery when she did and then stopped by my place to chat about flowers for Olivia's wedding."

"Wow, I don't know whether to be scared or flattered."

"Both probably. Be thankful we all care about you and want to know what prompted you to cut your family visit short. Also realize keeping secrets in a small town is hard work."

She pats Waldo on the head when he comes over to greet her. "Hey, big boy."

I head back into the kitchen to finish putting away the groceries. "Can I get you anything?"

"No, thanks, I've got to get back to the store. I told Cat I wouldn't be gone long." She unpacks my groceries from the last bag and stacks them on the counter. "You going to tell me what's going on or would you rather I mind my own business?"

I drop my head against the fridge door and sigh. "My family got on my nerves within a day, so I changed my flight and came home early."

"Sorry, family can be hard." She puts her hand on my shoulder.

I turn and force a tight smile. Rebecca is the last person I should complain to. She lost her parents, raises her special needs brother, and thought her sister was dead. "It's just drama. I overreact to their criticisms."

"Criticism from those closest to us tends to cut the deepest. That's not drama."

"That's part of the problem. I don't feel close to them most of the time. I'm like a changeling or something. I don't fit in with them. They're as baffled by me as I am by them."

"You may share DNA, but that doesn't mean you have to be alike. It took me many years to realize and accept that. I used to think Rachelle and I were polar opposites, but we're finding common ground. There's still a lot I don't know about her past, but we're learning to trust one another and open up. At least I think we are. Sometimes I'm still afraid she'll disappear again without a trace."

I rub her upper arm. "For what it's worth, Rachelle seems really happy here."

"I know, and it's just my old fears sneaking back in. Everything is so wonderful with Ian, and Drew and Rachelle are doing great. I worry something bad will ruin it."

"You deserve to be happy, and I have a feeling Ian will do everything in his power to ensure your continued happiness."

"He has made it a top priority." She winks. "I'm a lucky woman."

"You are, and I'm extremely envious of all my friends' love lives."

"You sound like Lucinda."

"She and I should get together and commiserate."

Rebecca leans against the counter and folds her arms. "Speaking of love lives…what's up with that picture of you and Holden Fox? You looked pretty chummy."

"Shows how much pictures lie. That picture was taken three months ago. He was in the middle of warning me off his son. I went there because Trevor invited me, and Holden went along with it to please his son, but he made it clear it wouldn't happen again."

"What an ass! Okay, we hate him."

I laugh and give her a hug. "Thanks, I needed that."

"Can I share with the girls or do you want it kept private? They're going to ask because we all saw the picture and recognized you."

"It's embarrassing, but at least I know their reactions are going to be more favorable than my family's."

She winces. "They saw the picture?"

"Oh yes, and if I kept my big mouth shut, they probably wouldn't have believed it was me. But I was feeling low and they were gossiping about a mystery woman. So, when my sister-in-law started making a connection between Holden and Mitch, and then remembered I had mentioned meeting Mitch," I roll my eyes, "classic case of karma coming back to bite me in the ass. I had bragged about meeting Mitch and then I admitted the mystery woman was me for the same reason. I wanted to fit in with them for a moment and make them see me as their equal."

"Stop beating yourself up. It's perfectly natural to want to fit in. I don't know your family, but if they're saying or doing anything to make you feel like less than you are, then they don't deserve you. They should be the ones trying to be more like you."

I lean against the counter next to her. "Thank you." I rest my head on her shoulder. "Why do I let them get to me?"

"Because our inner child always wants to please our parents and make them proud."

"They're not proud. They want me to move home, get married, and have children."

"They're aware what century this is, right?"

Laughing, I raise my head. "It's ridiculous. I know this, but it still bugs me. Just like it still upsets me when my grandmother basically calls me fat and won't let me eat bread."

Rebecca slowly turns to face me. "You're joking."

"I wish I was. She smacked the roll right out of my hand."

"I hope you threw it in her face. That's just stupid. You're not fat—not even close. You're beautiful. And even if you were, you'd still be beautiful." She slaps the top of the counter. "We hate her, too."

I tilt my head back and groan. "I can't hate her. She's my grandmother. I wanted to throw the whole bowl of rolls, but I did nothing because all I could envision was my family's reaction." I sigh. "I have a reputation for acting out."

"I've never been a fan of respecting my elders simply because they're old. People need to earn respect. She's not respecting you. I'm not saying you have to slap her in the face or anything. Although it sounds like someone should. You shouldn't have to be the one to always take the high road and suffer in silence, either."

"That's just it. It's taken me years to keep silent. As a teenager, I would have thrown the rolls and stormed out. I can't count the number of meals I left in the middle of. I threw my entire plate of food at my brother, Thomas, once because he told me I looked like a clown. I'd spent weeks designing and making one of my first outfits. I just snapped. He was teasing. That's what older brothers do. My parents were livid with me."

She squeezes my hand. "There's teasing, and there's cruelty. It's not funny if the person is hurt by what's being done or said. That's bullying."

"What if I told you I deleted one of my brother's college papers and he had to rewrite the entire thing after getting an extension from his professor. It could've kept him out of medical school." I pinch the bridge of my nose. "I never told anyone that before."

"I'd ask what he did to you?"

"He told his girlfriend at the time about a crush I had on a stupid boy. He went into my room and showed her how I'd written the boy's name with hearts around it all over the inside of my notebooks. Well, she was the older sister of one of the mean girls in school. Of course, she told her sister all about it. The sister then grabbed my notebook in front of the boy and the entire class and showed him. Everyone laughed. Middle school was hell."

"You remember the story about me setting my ex-boyfriend's belongings on fire, right? I think my reactions would've been much worse than yours. Your brothers are bullies, plain and simple."

"I'm really glad we're friends."

"Me too." She bumps my arm with hers. "I bet we can come up with a solid revenge plan. We could discuss it at the next book club."

I laugh out loud. "Please, no. I already feel much better talking to you."

"Good. And don't worry about that picture of you and Holden Fox. It'll blow over and I doubt anyone besides us will even know it was you."

Chapter Seven

The parasites will find another host soon.

I stare at Trevor's text for a minute or two. What obscure fact is he talking about now? At the risk of a twelve-year-old finding me stupid, I text back a question mark.

Paparazzi. They'll find another target to exploit.

Oh. I guess he saw the picture, too.

It's okay. Only a few people recognized me in the picture.

I don't want him thinking he's somehow responsible. He's just a kid and hardly responsible for the public scrutiny his father's profession brings to those around him. Poor Trevor has probably had to deal with it all his life.

Three little dots appear and disappear. Is he done texting? That's probably a good thing. His father probably won't be happy if Trevor and I start communicating a lot.

You haven't been out today, have you?

What does that mean? Oh no. Have they identified me?

The parasites know who you are. I'm sorry.

I squeeze my eyes shut.

It's not your fault.

How bad can it be? They won't care once they realize it's not true. I switch over to the internet and search an entertainment website.

"Mystery woman in Holden Fox's life identified!"
"Dress shop owner responsible for breaking Fox marriage!"
"Who is Kelly Tanner?"
"Samantha devastated by the betrayal!"

Pictures of me in town, through the window of my dress shop, and even a high school picture accompany the headlines. My stomach rolls, and I slap a hand over my mouth.

There's a picture of Trevor's mother with a tear-stained face. Another lie? Is it an old picture? Why would she be devastated if they're divorced? Besides the story isn't even true. There's nothing going on between Holden and me.

Trevor! What must the poor kid be going through? Here I am worrying about myself when it's his parents' lives plastered everywhere.

I switch back to my messages. *How are you holding up? Are you okay?*

Used to it. No big deal.

Truth?

Yeah. Old news.

Okay. Are you back in Texas?

Yeah.

School going okay? No one's giving you a tough time?

The dots linger. Is he still writing? Oh no, is he getting picked on because of this? Why isn't his father handling this? How dare those rotten kids bully Trevor!

I'm good. Don't worry.

Is he telling the truth? *Too late. If someone is bothering you, I want to know.*

I'm not sure exactly what I can do besides give his father and the school a piece of my mind, but I'll come up with something. I'm sure Rebecca will help me figure out a plan.

Relax. I don't care what they say.

So he is being bullied. Rotten, little demons.

Wait, is he talking about adults or kids? He could mean generally, like the trash the tabloids spout.

Bullying is never okay! Have you told anyone?

I ignore them and they stop. Means nothing. Promise.

I gnaw on my bottom lip. What should I do? Franny would give me Holden's number. He should know what's going on and fix it.

Does your father know?

About the picture? Yeah.

No, the bullying.

It's not important enough to bother him with. They're like buzzing flies. Annoying but harmless.

You're very wise for your age.

I know.

I laugh and send him a laughing emoji. I'm not going to keep harping on him about it, but I am going to make sure his father is aware.

Speaking of school. Gotta go. TTYL.

Okay. Have a good day!

You too.

I throw the covers back and climb out of bed. Nothing against Trevor, but this wasn't exactly the best way to wake up on my day off.

Pacing across my bedroom, I shoot off a text to Franny. *What's Holden's phone number?*

I grimace and wait for my phone to ring. There's no way she's going to let that slide. She'll have a million questions. Probably starting with why she should give out her husband's best friend's phone number. Considering he's a celebrity, she'll probably make me swear a few dozen times not to share it. Once I explain about Trevor, though, I'm sure she'll give it to me.

She texts me a phone number.

Okay…that was easy.

Thanks.

Give him hell. I'm here if you need me.

Well, dang, I guess Rebecca told her everything. My eyes get misty, and I sniff. I'm really lucky to have such good friends.

I dial his number before I lose my courage and pace once again. Trevor is what's important now.

The phone rings twice, and I scramble for a message to leave.

"Yeah?"

"Um…this is Kelly Tanner."

"I know."

How does he know? Did Franny tell him? Mitch. Mitch probably felt he needed to warn his buddy.

"You think I don't check out who my son talks to? I had your number the day of the wedding. I also know you've been texting him."

Fine. I guess I can't fault him for wanting to protect his son. It didn't occur to me he would read Trevor's texts, though.

"Then you know he's being bullied?"

"What!"

I stop pacing and frown at the phone. "I thought you said you saw the texts?"

"I said I knew about them, not that I read them. What the hell are you talking about?"

I huff out a breath and stare at the ceiling. "He wouldn't give me specifics, and he insisted it didn't bother him or mean anything, but it shouldn't be happening at all." I recount the gist of our text conversation.

His drawn-out sigh echoes over the phone.

"I'll take care of it. Thanks for telling me."

"You're welcome. I care about Trevor. He's a great kid."

"Yeah, he is. Listen, about the picture. If you keep your mouth shut and don't give them any ammunition, they'll lose interest."

"I have no intention of speaking to anyone."

What does he think? I'm going to go blabbing about him or something?

"Good."

"Goodbye, Mr. Fox." I disconnect before he replies. Is he worried about my reaction to the media frenzy, or is he worried about his own reputation? Does he think I'll tell everyone what a jerk he is?

He doesn't seem overly concerned about the fact the media is flat-out lying.

Wouldn't it be better to tell the truth so everyone stops speculating?

Or would saying anything just perpetuate the story and peak people's interest?

The media talked for months about the custody battle. He's probably hoping silence will keep it from being dredged up again. Although I don't remember him commenting during that entire ordeal, either.

I'm sure he has publicists and managers directing him what to do or not do.

I set my phone down on my nightstand and huff out a breath. At least the store is closed today. What are the chances a new story will break before tomorrow and everyone will forget about me?

Chapter Eight

"Wasn't sure you were going to show up for book club today." Sally grins at me from the entrance to Franny's living room.

I wave my hand around the room. "If it wasn't for these daring ladies, I doubt I would've. They braved the remaining paparazzi to sneak me out of my home and here to Franny and Mitch's house."

Lucinda snickers and crosses her legs. Her navy velour leggings and ivory cowl neck sweater look not only stylish but comfortable. "You should've seen Kelly's face when Franny, Olivia, Rebecca, and I arrived at her house and donned our disguises."

"Trench coats, dark sunglasses, and scarves to cover our hair." Olivia sits next to Lucinda and hands her a glass of wine. "It was so much fun. They didn't know which one of us to follow when we left the house and separated. I felt like a spy."

"It was fun. We should do it again just for the hell of it." Rebecca clinks her glass to Olivia's.

"I think they're finally losing interest in me. There have been less and less lurking around each day. I feel like I've been held hostage over the past week."

"Hey, don't forget Kerry's and my role. We helped, too." Monica walks in dressed in a purple turtleneck sweater and jeans and sits in one of the chairs flanking the enormous fireplace.

"How could I ever forget the two of you blocking the photographers with your cars? I swear it was like a movie! They had this elaborate plan and executed it perfectly." I smile and raise my glass. "Here's to the book club ladies. If I'm ever in another bind, I know exactly who to call."

"Damn straight. We kick ass." Rebecca raises her glass high.

Lucinda chuckles and tilts her glass at Rebecca. "It was Rebecca's idea. Although her original plan involved a little more violence. She wanted us to storm over there and knock them all unconscious before escorting you to Franny's house."

"Lucinda came up with the disguises after pointing out we'd probably all be arrested for assault." Olivia points to Monica. "Then Monica suggested using cars to delay them giving chase."

Kerry and Tina stroll in the room. They're both wearing black leggings and jewel-toned, long, buttoned shirts.

"Oh, are we talking about Kelly's great escape? I was terrified at the time, but now it all seems so exciting."

"Were you terrified when you drove over the curb and sidewalk?" Monica shakes her head. "I thought Kerry was going to drive right over one of those photographers."

"I might have gotten a little overzealous at that point, but he had a motorcycle. I had to block him from going after them."

Franny comes in and fills the plates of appetizers on the coffee table. "Mitch got a tad upset with me when I recounted our adventures. I had to endure a lecture about safety and promise to run any future plans to avoid paparazzi by him first."

"I'm sorry I missed all the excitement." Tina sips at her water. "I have an announcement I've been dying to tell you all. I wish Barbara and Aggie were here, too, but I just can't wait."

I laugh. "Good. I'm really sick of being the topic of conversation. Share your news with us."

I can't keep running the store from a distance. Without Lenore's help, I would've had to close. At least my business hasn't suffered. The gawkers and celebrity hungry people shop in my store hoping to get an inside scoop or something. The added income will help pay for Lenore's additional hours.

Tina bites her lip and scans the room. "I'm pregnant."

Monica jumps up with a squeal and lunges over to give Tina a hug. Lucinda claps her hands with a giant grin on her face. Franny and Olivia both cover their mouths with their hands as tears fill their eyes. Sally drags a tissue from her sleeve and dabs her eyes. Kerry joins Monica and Tina in a group hug, and they sway back and forth.

One by one we all join in.

Monica wipes her eyes. "The first baby in our little group. Well, Olivia has the twins, Barbara has Joey. And Tina has her stepdaughter, Hope. But this is the first time one of us has gotten pregnant since we formed the book club."

I've only been part of the group for about a year, but I feel like I've known these women for ages. They welcomed me with no hesitation. I dig the heels of my hands into my eyes to stem the flow of tears.

"We're all going to look a fright. If Mitch walks in here, he'll think something is terribly wrong." Lucinda walks over to her purse and hands out tissues to everyone.

Franny waves her tissue in the air. "If Mitch walks in here, he'll turn right around and run in the other direction."

Sally plants her hands on her hips and sniffs. "That's a typical male reaction. They don't know how to handle a bunch of crying women."

"Very few men know how to deal with women period." Rebecca sits down and crosses her legs. "Some of us have gotten rather lucky, though, and Tina's one of them. Congratulations."

"We need to share a toast." Lucinda picks up her glass.

"Wait, I think I've got some sparkling juice." Franny points a finger at her sister. "Hold that thought. I'll be right back."

Monica refills her glass. "I was wondering why you were drinking water." She shakes her head at Tina. "You're sneaky. You haven't been drinking coffee lately, either. I didn't connect the dots."

Tina holds her hands over her cheeks. "It's been so hard to keep the secret. I wanted to tell everyone even complete strangers."

"You should be excited. Shout it to the rooftops." Olivia winks. "I remember when you started dating Ron. My marriage to Ryan was on the rocks. Look at both of us now. I'm planning my wedding to Luke and you're going to have a baby. Hope must be over the moon."

"She is! She's going to be the best big sister. She's been helping come up with baby names. She reads the pregnancy books with me and has made lists of things we need to do to prepare for when the baby comes."

"How's Ron handling becoming a daddy again?"

Tina shakes her head at Kerry. "He's a sweetheart, of course. Couldn't be more thrilled and prouder. But he's worried about everything. I swear he'd put me in a giant bubble if he could. I have to text or call him whenever I go somewhere and let him know I've arrived at my destination. He doesn't want me lifting a finger—I don't mind that part a bit."

"Enjoy every minute of it." Rebecca grabs some cheese and crackers from the charcuterie board. "You'll need your rest as the pregnancy advances and when the baby comes."

"Found it." Franny waves the bottle of sparkling juice. "Sorry it took me so long. It was in the back of the cupboard." She pours Tina a glass and one for herself and drops a couple of ice cubes into hers.

Lucinda stands. "To Tina, Ron, Hope, and baby on the way! May your pregnancy be effortless and the delivery a breeze."

"Good luck with that." Sally cackles before she swallows a long sip of wine.

Monica clicks her glass against Tina's. "To beautiful babies and beautiful moms."

"Here's to lots of family and friends to help through it all." Olivia grins. "I'd like to sign up for babysitting duty now. I could use a baby fix. My boys don't like to snuggle as much anymore."

"Uh oh. Luke better watch out."

Lucinda wags her finger at her sister. "Bite your tongue, Franny. I'm in the midst of planning their wedding. No surprise babies until after it's done."

I pluck another chip from the bowl and swipe it through the cheesy dip. "I'm not going to tell you no babies; that's completely your choice. I will say your dress would need some serious adjustments, though." Actually, considering her wedding is only a couple months away, it's doubtful she'd be showing much even if she got pregnant right away.

"I said baby fix, people. I did not say I wanted another baby. Yet." Olivia laughs and pops a meatball into her mouth.

Mitch appears in the doorway. "Hi, ladies. Sorry to interrupt. Franny, can I talk to you for a minute?"

She frowns and makes her way over to him while we all pretend not to be curious about what's going on. He whispers something in her ear and hands her his phone. She stares at it a moment before turning to look at me.

Oh no, what could it be now?

Franny nibbles on her lip. "Kelly, could you come with me into the kitchen for a minute?"

I close my eyes and sigh. "Just tell me. I'd rather everyone know at once."

I'm sure they'll find out anyway and this will save me any retelling. It can't be another picture. I haven't been near Holden Fox.

Mitch squeezes Franny's hand. "Samantha Fox released a statement."

What could that possibly have to do with me?

Franny walks over to stand next to my chair. She puts her hand on my shoulder. "The vile woman claims you're the reason her marriage to Holden ended."

How is that possible? She can just outright lie?

Mitch takes a few steps into the room. "She put on quite a performance. It might be her best acting job ever. She broke down sobbing in the middle of her little speech and had to be walked off the stage."

"Why? Why would she do that? It's not true. I'm not having an affair with Holden Fox."

Mitch scowls. "Publicity and to manipulate Holden."

"What a bitch!" Rebecca walks over and takes my hand.

This is a nightmare!

I stare at Mitch. "People won't believe her, will they?"

His grimace says it all. Of course they will.

"You'll get through this." Franny rubs my arm.

Lucinda scoots closer to me. "You can sue her. I'd have to watch the video to hear exactly what she says, but if she's spreading lies about you, that's defamation of character."

Mitch clears his throat. "She was very careful not to name Kelly or give any specifics." He rubs his hand over the back of his neck. "I'm sorry, Kelly. It's not fair to you. You could make your own statement."

"Wouldn't that be case of she said she said?" Monica looks at Lucinda, who just nods.

"The truth would still be out there. People who know you will believe you, not her."

I glance at Tina and give her a small smile. The people in this room would believe me, but what about everyone else? The residents of Granite Cove? My customers? My family?

Oh God! My family! They'll probably hear this, too.

My parents had been less than happy when the picture came out, but they had believed me when I told them it was a misinterpretation of an innocent meeting. What will they think when they hear her lies?

Chapter Nine

If you're going to hide out from the media and pretty much everyone else, this isn't a bad place to do it. Ribbons of peach, pink, and lavender paint the sky. The setting sun glistens over the lake. The view from Franny and Mitch's guest room is picture perfect. I reach for my phone to snap a picture of the view and post it on my social media account. Nope, can't do that anymore. I closed all my accounts.

The hate messages from rabid fans clinched that decision. I toyed with canceling them in the past. Falling down the rabbit hole of social media was a big time suck, and the negative content people spew on a regular basis was such a downer. I kept them to stay current with family and friends. At least that's what I told myself repeatedly when the urge to cancel arose.

Someone knocks on the guest room door. Franny is probably checking in on me again. How many people would insist I stay with them when a crisis hits? Sure, they feel slightly responsible since I only came into contact with Holden because of them. Even though I've reassured them repeatedly it's not their fault, Franny still gets that sorry expression on her face when she looks at me. Of course, that could just be pity.

"Come in."

Turning away from the view, I glance down at my flannel pajamas and shrug. They're old but comfy. Franny won't mind. She doesn't care much about clothes, and she's not the judgy type.

Holden walks in, and my stomach drops to the floor. What is he doing here? Why is he in my room while I'm in my ratty old pajamas with my hair in a messy bun and not a trace of makeup on my face? Why the hell didn't Franny warn me?

"Hey."

I rub the space between my eyebrows. I don't need this right now.

"What are you doing here?"

"Franny said you were upset about all the media coverage." He rubs the back of his neck and smirks. "Actually she said I needed to haul my ass up here to Granite Cove and fix it."

That sounds like something she would do and say. Although I really wish she would've consulted me first.

"I don't see how you showing up in Granite Cove will help matters. It'll only add fuel to the ridiculous rumors."

"I pointed that out. Which is why I flew into Boston and drove up so the chances of anyone knowing I'm here are nil."

His gaze wanders over me and narrows. If he makes some criticism about my appearance, I'm going to throw something at him.

He walks across the room and stops in front of me.

I search around for something heavy to brain him with. A lamp? No, it might be expensive, and I don't want to upset Franny or Mitch.

That ceramic coaster of the New Hampshire coastline might get my point across. I'm sure I can afford to replace that—even though my sales have tanked this week because I had to close the store for a couple of days.

"Angel?"

My gaze snaps back to his. "What did you call me?"

"You're real."

I roll my eyes. "Of course I'm real. I'm standing right here with emotions and everything. What the hell is your problem?"

"I thought I imagined you." He stares into my eyes. "New York. Fashion week. Thirteen years ago."

Bollocks! He remembers.

Now? He remembers now? I stare at the door behind him. Running out of the room won't help anything. I glance at the bathroom door. Would letting him think I have a bathroom emergency be worse?

I could deny it altogether.

"My memory is a bit hazy from that night."

I snort. "You were blind drunk." I slap my hand over my mouth. So much for denial.

A slow grin stretches over his face. "It *is* you."

He rubs the back of his finger over my cheek before I swat it away.

"Stop it. What are you doing?"

"Seeing if it's as soft as I remember." His gaze wanders over my face like he's memorizing every inch. "You didn't have any war paint on then, either. It was so refreshing after being surrounded by women covered in makeup and product all the time."

"I was young and too exhausted to care at the time." I'd been working insane, unsustainable hours as an intern for a sadistic fashion designer.

His fingers toy with a strand of my hair. "Your hair was darker then, but it was falling down then, too. You had a pencil sticking out of the top."

"Convenience. I was always losing pens and pencils, so I'd stick one in my bun."

His gaze lands on my lips, and I swallow.

"Those lips have haunted me for years." His thumb presses against my bottom lip. "I need to know if it's as good as I remember."

His head slowly lowers, and my mouth goes dry.

I should smack him.

Why aren't I smacking him?

I should move away at the very least.

His lips brush over mine.

My breath shudders at the back of my throat.

He cups my face in his hands and his lips kiss mine. My eyes drift closed.

The tip of his nose skims mine as his tongue traces the seam of my lips. Pliant, I open for him.

His lips and tongue caress mine softly at first but grow bolder with each pass.

I sway toward him.

"Might be better than I remember." His soft drawl permeates my numb brain as his lips kiss my cheek.

I open my eyes. "More experience."

His face hovers inches above mine. "Shame about that. I envy every single man that's tasted these lips."

A memory teases the back of my mind. "Wasn't that a line in a movie?"

He grins and shrugs as I step away from him. "It was a good one. Doesn't make it any less true."

How could I forget Holden Fox is simply a charming playboy?

"Right, it's so true I never saw you again after our only kiss and you didn't recognize me when you did see me."

I whirl away and squeeze my eyes closed. Now I sound like I've been pining after him for years while he's flitted from one woman to the next. Apparently while he's been married to Trevor's mother the entire time. No wonder the media eat up her tearful press releases. Why aren't they maligning him? Because he's a man?

"I thought I'd imagined you, and it *has* been years. Why didn't you say anything?"

I shoot him a dark glance as I stride over and collapse into one of the armchairs facing the French doors. "Why would I? If you recall, you were being a jerk. And what was I supposed to say? You have enough women simpering over you. I won't be one of them."

"You certainly couldn't be accused of that." He sits in the chair next to me.

Now what? What is he thinking?

"Why did you kiss me? We can hardly deny any involvement now. Although a kiss is nothing to what they and your ex-wife are accusing me of."

"They would never have believed any statement denying it anyway. As for Samantha, we were married in name only for Trevor's sake. She's only milking this for the publicity and her barely existent career. I divorced her when he was still a baby. She's never been a mother to him.

I finally got full custody this year after handing her a small fortune. All she cares about is money and fame."

"Poor Trevor."

"Yeah, I've protected him from her as much as I can, but her neglect and manipulations are hard to explain away to a kid."

"How is he? I assume he's seen her performance?"

"Says he's fine. He's more worried about what it's doing to you. You've made quite an impression on him."

"He has more empathy and wisdom than most adults I know. You've obviously done something right raising him."

"I'm not sure I can take credit for that. I think he might have been born that way."

I stare at his reflection in the glass. The sun has set and darkness lies over the lake.

If what he's saying is true, then he's not a cheater. How can she get away with everything she's said about him? Why does he let her?

Trevor? But if he has full custody now, why doesn't he set the record straight?

"Why do you let her get away with it? If you've been divorced for years? This isn't the first time she's made a public statement painting you as a villain."

I, like most of the world, thought he was only recently divorced. Samantha Fox has given interviews before making Holden out to be a heartless, cheating husband. I found one story after another when I did a misguided search after her statement.

"I spent a lot of time and money in the beginning combating her theatrics. People believe what they want to believe. She's a convincing actress. It's her personality and self-destructive tendencies that ruin her career."

He's right. People believe what they want. The pictures and videos are edited to tell a tale that sells. It doesn't seem to matter if it's all a lie.

When I saw the footage and the photos of Holden and me, I half believed it was real—and I was there and knew the truth.

"So you just let her get away with it?"

"If I fight her, I give her what she wants—more media attention. For

Trevor's sake and my own, it's better to keep quiet and let the story die a natural death."

"Okay. It doesn't seem fair, but I understand." I don't want to hurt Trevor. I guess I'll have to hide out here with Franny and Mitch for another day or two until the wolves stop surrounding my home and business.

I suppose it's wrong to wish for someone else's life to implode and take over the news. How about something harmless but newsworthy? Not a natural disaster or anything, but maybe a celebrity divorce or something.

"Why don't you come back to Texas with me? Trevor would love to see you, and it would give everything a chance to die down here."

I stare at him blankly. Go to Texas with him? My mouth is slightly agape. I snap it closed and glance away.

"Franny said you haven't been able to go to your store, so it's not like you'd be missing work. Do you still design clothing, too? You could bring your stuff with you. I've got the room at the ranch. It's the least I can do since this is happening to you because of me."

Guilty conscience?

It's his ex-wife's fault, really. Well, she's perpetuating it and making it worse. It's his celebrity that makes anyone give a dang.

Still, I can't go to Texas with him.

"It's kind of you to offer, but it's unnecessary. As you said, the story will go away, eventually."

"Yeah, but if you get out of town, it'll go faster."

"Not if they find out I'm with you."

"They already believe the worst. Why not take advantage of it? If they're going to punish us for the crime, we might as well enjoy the time." He winks and grins.

"You're not seriously suggesting we have an affair because they already accused us of having one?"

"At least admit you're tempted."

I open my mouth to tell him to go to hell but frown instead as a tingling begins in the pit of my stomach.

How insane would it be if I said yes? Everyone already thinks the worst of me anyway even though none of it is true.

"All I'm agreeing to is Texas. Getting out of town does sound like a good idea. And since technically it is your fault...No one would give a dang about who I have dinner with." I waggle my finger at him. "But if you think for one moment I'm going to fall into your bed simply for the heck of it because everyone believes I already have, then you're out of your mind."

He leans across the space between the chairs. "Angel, when I get you into my bed—and make no mistake, it's going to happen—it won't be because of anyone else."

Chapter Ten

Clear, blue sky shines in every direction. The small clump of trees at the top of the hill provides decent shade from the sun. Trevor's horse's tail swishes away a fly. The scents of horse, leather, and nature envelop me. The sprawling two-story ranch house is down below. The barn and various outbuildings resemble a small town from up here.

"You're a natural rider, Kelly. Isn't she, Dad?"

Holden's gaze rakes over me, lingering on my hip and butt. "Sure is."

I look away. I'm not sure what I expected when I agreed to go with Holden to Texas. I didn't exactly think it through. My impulsive nature raised its head. There's something about the land here. It's beautiful, of course, but it's haunting, too. The rolling hills echo with a past that ensnared me from the first moment I laid eyes on the land. I've only been here a couple of days, but I feel like I've lived a lifetime here. I've never believed in reincarnation before, but I can understand how someone can believe it after the connection I feel here.

"Sandy has taken a liking to you, too." Trevor nods his head toward the horse.

I smile at him. "Sandy likes the bribes I've been giving her. She has a fondness for apples."

The palomino lifts her head and her ears twitch backward as if she understands what I'm saying and expects an apple.

Trevor and Holden both chuckle. Their laugh is similar. Holden's is more of a rumble, but the similarity is there.

"We should head back. You'll be sore later if we don't. You're not accustomed to long rides in the saddle—yet."

My cheeks heat.

I jerk the reins to follow Holden and Trevor back to the ranch.

Trevor's horse trots over so I'm once again between Trevor and Holden. "Annie is making enchiladas for dinner. Did you know they originated with the Aztecs?"

"No, I didn't. Annie is a wonderful cook. I'm going to miss her and her cooking when I go back home."

"You're staying for the rest of the week, though, right?"

Trevor's enthusiasm at my arrival and in showing me his home has been a comfort. I'll miss him when it's time to leave.

"Lenore and my new assistant, Patty, are watching the store. I can't leave them to handle everything for much longer." They've been giving me regular updates and Rebecca stops in daily to check on things for me. Her sister, Rachelle, does, too. I wanted to hire her, but I think the publicity scared her away.

"A few more days shouldn't make a difference."

I glance Holden's way.

He's been subtle in his attempts at seduction. Nothing blatant, just long looks and lingering touches at unexpected moments. His hand resting on my back. His fingers trailing down my arm. His thumb brushing over the pulse point in my wrist again and again. His hands gripping my waist when he helped me into the saddle.

Yet he hasn't kissed me again or talked about sharing his bed.

The saddle creaks as I shift. I know what he's doing, and it's working because I can't stop thinking about him or wondering when he'll kiss me again. Knowing doesn't make the anticipation stop. It's annoying he's so good at seduction and that I'm falling for it. I should know better.

I do know better.

Holden Fox wasn't voted sexiest man alive more than once for nothing.

He's probably right that I'll end up in his bed, eventually. The question is will I survive it with my heart intact?

* * *

"You're a nanny now? If you want to be a nanny, come home and be one to your brothers' kids. Brian is looking for a new one."

"She doesn't need to be a nanny. She needs her own kids."

I pinch the bridge of my nose as my mother and grandmother bicker back and forth over my life. Why did I answer the phone?

I plop down on the edge of the bed and lie down staring at the ceiling. Holden was right about my muscles aching. The bath helped somewhat.

"Come home, Kelly Anne."

Grand-Mére chimes in. "Yes, we'll find you a proper man to marry. One with kids already. You're getting too old to have any of your own."

My mother sucks in a harsh breath. "What do you mean? Women these days are having children in their forties and even fifties."

"Hush, CiCi. I don't have that long to wait. Don't you want to see your daughter walk down the aisle? I do. Kelly Anne, it's time to come home. No more gallivanting around babysitting that actor's kids."

"One kid and I'm not his nanny."

"I thought you said she was his nanny."

"No, Candace said that. Or maybe it was Suzanne. It doesn't matter. Her picture was taken because of her relationship with the son, not the father. We all assumed it was because she's his new nanny. It made the most sense. What else could it be?"

Of course they assume I'm Trevor's new nanny. I told my sister-in-law I talk with Trevor more than Holden so she would stop texting me asking questions about him. So they automatically make the assumption I'm now a nanny.

"How old is this son?"

I grimace and shake my head. "He's twelve, Grand-Mére. Don't get any ideas."

Mom sighs loudly. I can picture her throwing her hands up in the air in defeat. "I don't understand any of this. If you're not the nanny, why are you with them in Texas?"

I really, *really* wish I hadn't told them that. When am I going to learn to lie? Lenore had only told my mother I was away when she called looking for me. I could have and should have lied and told her I was on vacation in Paris or something. Of course, if I had answered the first dozen calls or text messages she left me, then she wouldn't have called Lenore in the first place and wouldn't have known I wasn't in Granite Cove.

"I'm here because I needed to get away from all the craziness and paparazzi. So I said yes when Holden asked."

"Why would he ask you to go to Texas?"

"Are you sure you're not the nanny?"

"No, I'm not the nanny! Holden and I *are* dating." There, let them chew on that for a while. Candace and Suzanne will lose their minds when they hear.

A shadow falls over me.

Holden stands next to the bed, staring down at me.

Please, *please*, tell me he didn't hear any of that.

He folds his arms over his chest and lifts one blond eyebrow.

"Mom, Grand-Mére, I have to go. I'll call you later." Their protests die abruptly when I end the call.

"I can explain."

Can I, though?

Is he mad?

Oh Lord! He doesn't think I've been telling everyone we're a couple, does he?

Except that's pretty much what I just did. My mother and grandmother will tell the whole family. My sisters-in-law, or at least one or two in particular, will tell everyone else.

"I plead insanity!"

Chapter Eleven

Holden's lips twitch, and I swear his eyes sparkle. I chomp down on my bottom lip and prop myself up on my elbows.

"You don't know what my family is like. They wouldn't listen."

"Your phone was on speaker. I heard plenty."

"Oh."

He smiles. Okay, he's not mad.

But then again, he doesn't realize what the ramifications of telling my family something like that means.

The story won't die now. My family will authenticate it with their thoughtless gossip. The situation could get worse.

So much worse. Suzanne loves the spotlight. She'll tell them anything they want to hear. What horrible tales will she spread about me?

"Why do you look like you're going to throw up? It's no big deal. You told your mother we're dating. Now she'll stop badgering you about moving home and getting married to some guy they set you up with, right?"

"You heard that, too? How long were you standing there?"

"Why? What else did they say?"

I close my eyes and drop my head back to the bed. "I'm not

repeating any of it, and you wouldn't be smiling if you had any idea how my impulsive declaration will snowball. Everyone in my family will know. In fact, it's been a few minutes, so they probably already do. Everyone they know will know by the end of the day. This could get very bad."

The mattress dips, and my eyes shoot open.

Holden lies down next to me with his head propped on his hand. His elbow digs into the silver-and-cream comforter. The green of his eyes remind me of a lush forest after a light rain.

"I stopped caring about what people I don't know think a long time ago. You can't control it, so don't waste your time worrying about it."

"Easier said than done."

"What's the worst they can do? Tell people we're having an affair? They already think that."

"But it's not true."

"Yet. It isn't true yet." He presses his lips to mine. His tongue delves into my mouth in a passionate kiss.

I loop my arms around his neck. I don't want to think anymore. I just want to feel.

"I'm really glad you took my suggestion to have a bath." His fingers loosen the sash on my robe as his lips place kisses across my cheek to my neck and shoulder.

"Me too. It helped."

"I'm glad about that, too, but I was referring to the easier access." He parts my robe and stares down at me like a starving man before a feast.

"You're so beautiful, Angel."

"That's not a generic term you use when you can't remember a woman's name, is it?"

He pauses above me and frowns. "I've never called anyone but you that. You were my dream angel. I thought I imagined you."

"Oh, well then, please proceed."

He chuckles, and his lips explore the curves of my shoulder and collarbone. "Hold that thought." He pushes off the mattress to stand next to it, staring down at me. "I have to run to my room for a moment because I wasn't prepared for this. Unless you have a condom? He scans the room."

"Um...actually there's one in my purse." I point to it sitting on the upholstered bench at the end of the bed. "It's an old habit. My brothers insisted I always have one when I left for college. They would dump out my purse to check anytime they saw me so I started carrying one at all times."

"In that case, let me just lock the door. Trev went to bed a while ago, but I'd prefer not to have any interruptions."

How could I forget about Trevor? What will he think if he finds out I slept with his father? Will he be upset? Will he hate me?

The lock clicks, and I drag my gaze back to Holden when he walks toward me.

"Now, what's wrong?"

"I don't want to upset Trevor."

"I told you. He went to bed. He sleeps like the dead."

So he intends to keep this from him or it's just a one-time thing, or both?

It's not like I'm expecting a commitment—we barely know each other. All we have so far is attraction.

I yank my robe together and sit up all the way. Holden drops his head and sits next to me on the bed.

"Talk to me. What's going through your head?"

"Trevor is very smart, and I'm a terrible liar. He'll figure it out, you know. You may think you can keep it a secret, but—"

"I don't have many secrets from him. This won't be one of them."

I stare at him with my mouth agape. "What does that mean?"

"It means he already knows I'm attracted to you and he knows I planned to make the rumors a reality."

"You discussed this with him? You discussed me? You told your twelve-year-old son you planned to get me in your bed?"

"Technically, this is *your* bed."

"Not one bit funny."

"I didn't discuss having sex with you if that's what you're worried about. I did, however, make sure he was okay with me dating you. I don't allow anyone into our lives without talking to him first, and since you're friends with him, it was even more important. He's fine with it, *by* the way." He kisses my shoulder. "More than fine, actually. He's the one who helped Annie make those cupcakes for you. He also lectured me about treating you respectfully."

I drop my head to his shoulder.

Am I being my typical impulsive self? It's not just Holden and me to consider. Trevor has enough drama in his life. I don't want to add to it.

"I can feel how hard your brain is working, but unless you actually speak those thoughts out loud, I can't help."

"I'm trying to curb my impulsive tendencies and think this out before I act."

"You're impulsive?"

"See, if you knew me better, you'd know impulsivity is one of my flaws."

"Says who?"

"My family. I've lost count of the number of lectures I've had over the years about not thinking my decisions through. They call me impulsive when disaster doesn't strike following my actions and reckless when it does."

"Give me an example."

"Of my impulsivity?"

Holden nods and puts his arm around my shoulders.

"I moved to Granite Cove by randomly picking a place on a map."

He chuckles. "Okay, it seems to have worked out for you, though. I see nothing wrong with that."

"I kissed a drunken stranger in an elevator when I was supposed to be running errands for my boss and got fired."

He grimaces. "Explains why I couldn't find you the next day. When no one could tell me where or even who you were, I thought I made you up in my less than sober imaginings."

"You searched for me?"

"You were so sweet and refreshing. I couldn't get you or our kiss out of my head."

"That's nice to hear, but it was a long time ago. We're different people now, and I'm trying to be responsible since it's not just us to consider."

"I appreciate how much you worry about Trev. And I get you want to be sure. We can slow things down. We don't have to jump into bed until you're ready." He kisses my cheek. "Let's take the next few days to get to know one another before you head back to Granite Cove."

"Thank you, I think it's for the best."

"For the record, I don't think impulsivity is a flaw. We wouldn't have met either time if you weren't. A little spontaneity keeps life interesting."

"You say that now but wait until my decisions lead to your life exploding and then let's see how you feel."

"Bring it on, Angel. I doubt there's anything you could do that could make my life any crazier than it's been. Besides, I'm the reason your life exploded recently, remember?"

"True, and don't think I won't remind you of that if I do something that leads to disaster."

"Fair enough."

Chapter Twelve

"You're entirely too good at this game for a twelve-year-old." My solid-colored balls are scattered all over the pool table. Trevor only has one striped ball and, of course, the eight-ball remaining.

Trevor shrugs. "It's just geometry."

"That explains it then. I suck at math."

He laughs and points to the yellow ball. "That shot is simple."

"Says the little pool hustler." I line up my shot with the cue ball and yellow ball.

Holden paces over by the bar in the corner while he talks on the phone. A bubbly feeling invades my chest. It's been an idyllic couple of days. We spend the day with Trevor, riding, playing games, or just hanging out. After he goes to bed, Holden and I lie in each other's arms talking. He hasn't pushed for intimacy. Other than some heated make-out sessions, our involvement is fairly innocent.

The cue ball hits the yellow ball with a solid thwack. It speeds toward the corner pocket but slows on its approach. The ball teeters at the hole. A simple hip bump would knock it in. Heck, I could probably blow on it and it would fall in.

Sighing, I rest the bottom of my stick on the ground. "Pool is so not my game."

"The entire fam is on their way over." Holden scans the pool table as he walks past. "If it makes you feel any better, my sister and I are the only ones he doesn't beat every time."

His entire family is coming here? Now?

He told me his parents live nearby. I wondered if I would meet them while I was here because according to Trevor, they either come here or Holden and Trevor go there multiple times per week. But, since I'm leaving tomorrow, I figured I wouldn't meet them.

It looks like I'm not only going to meet them, but also Holden's two sisters. What has he told them about me?

They must have seen all the publicity.

"Cool. Gram said she wanted to meet Kelly."

I nibble on my bottom lip.

"Trev, go tell Annie they'll be more of us for dinner."

Holden rubs my back. "It'll be fine. My family doesn't get wrapped up in the celebrity drama. They've learned to ignore it. They know we're dating and they want to meet you. We'll have dinner and chill. No big deal."

Right, no big deal. Easy for him to say. He's not the one meeting the family for the first time.

I've met the families of guys I've dated before. There were no catastrophes.

Unless you count Don's mother, Tammy. The day we met, she asked if I was pregnant. She couldn't fathom any other reason for her son to bring me to meet her. Turns out, he had gotten a girl pregnant when they were both in high school. It would have been fine, except he never told me he had a kid he never saw. Not exactly an example of upstanding moral character. The relationship ended soon after that visit.

"Okay, I just wish I had a little more warning to prepare."

"What's to prepare? We'll chat. We'll eat. Have some laughs. Nothing complicated you need to prepare for."

What a typical guy response. Do they really never worry about making a good impression on someone they meet? Especially when it's meeting the family of a guy you're dating?

I smooth my sweater and jeans. Should I run upstairs and change?

What he's describing is casual. He's in jeans, too. I don't want to be overdressed. What about makeup? I should at least put some on.

"I'm going to run upstairs—"

The tread of multiple people coming down the stairs ends any possibility of disappearing upstairs and putting on makeup.

I run my hands over my hair and tuck any strays behind my ears or back into my braid.

An older woman with blonde hair swinging over her shoulders appears first. She looks to be in her fifties or early sixties. This must be Holden's mother. She's wearing jeans, too. Good, I'm glad I didn't change.

A tall man with silver-streaked blond hair follows behind her.

With a wide smile, she embraces Holden and glances my way. "You must be Kelly."

I shake her offered hand, smiling. "It's so nice to meet you."

"I'm Lily and this is my husband, Bo. Our daughters, Tori and Tess, are upstairs with Trevor. They'll all be along in a minute." She smiles at Holden. "I brought over a pie for dessert."

"Apple?"

Lily rubs Holden's shoulder. "Would I bring you anything else?" She leans closer to me as if she's imparting a secret. "It's his favorite."

"Good to know."

"Holden tells us you hail from New Hampshire?" Bo rocks on his heels with his hands in the front pockets of his jeans.

"Yes, I moved there a couple years ago. I grew up in Chicago."

"A city girl?" A blonde, younger version of Lily walks across the room. "I'm Tess."

I shake her hand. "Kelly, and yes, I guess I was a city girl for most of my life. Granite Cove has converted me into a small-town girl, though."

"I might do the opposite and change from a small-town girl into a city girl. I've been thinking about moving to Houston or even Dallas."

"You're only saying that because you broke up with Cameron again." A tall, tan woman with a cowboy hat waltzes across the room.

Tess plants her hands on her hips. "Cameron has nothing to do with it. I need opportunities this hick town will never give me. You'll never understand because you barely set foot off the ranch."

"Girls, now is not the time. Tori, say hello to Holden's guest, Kelly."

She nods in my direction. I smile back.

Trevor walks down the stairs carrying a platter. "Annie whipped up some guacamole and chips." He places the platter on the bar. We all gravitate over while Holden makes drinks for everyone. Tess and Tori stay behind except to call out their orders when asked. They whisper furiously at each other.

Lily scoops up some guac on a chip and pops it into her mouth. "Annie makes the best guacamole. Tell us about Granite Cove. We visited Holden and Trev over the summer, and it was a charming town. Quintessential New England. Busy, though."

"I'll say. It took us over half an hour to travel less than a mile through town. Cars and people everywhere." Bo tilts his cowboy hat back on his head and digs back into the chips.

"Summer can get pretty busy at times, but it's not the norm. Most of the year, Granite Cove is fairly quiet with no traffic worries."

Holden hands me a glass of wine. "We were there in the spring for the wedding and recently in the fall. It's nowhere near as busy."

"Rack 'em up, Trev. I'm going to beat you this time." Tess grabs a pool stick from the holder on the wall.

"There's always a first time." Trevor grins and fills the triangle on the table with the balls.

Tori leans against the bar next to me and watches them play.

"Do you live on the ranch with your parents or is it a different one Tess was referring to?"

She gives me a sideways glance and tilts her bottle of beer back to drink. "Same one."

"That must be nice—working on the family ranch."

She gives a curt nod and glances away.

Okay, she's either not big on conversation or she's upset after her talk with Tess. Or maybe it's me.

Lilly and Bo slide into a pair of bar stools farther down while they chat with Holden. He sends me a wink and folds his arms over the bar as he leans toward his parents.

I can't just walk away from her. That would be rude, wouldn't it?

"You're leaving tomorrow, right?"

"Um...yes." What should I read into that? Is she happy I'm going?

"Any plans to return?"

"To come back to Texas? I don't know. I'd like to. I've had a wonderful time, and it's so beautiful here."

She stares at me silently. I take a sip of wine and set it on the bar.

"People try to use my brother all the time."

What is she saying? Is she accusing me of using Holden for something?

"I'm not one of them if that's what you're implying."

"So you're not hoping some of the spotlight will rub off on you? You're an aspiring fashion designer, aren't you? Seems to me dating a celebrity and having access to the people he knows would be quite the boon for a woman in your position."

"I'm a dress shop owner. The only designing I do is for my customers. I no longer have any aspirations to become a fashion designer. I tried that route for many years and concluded it wasn't for me. I have no desire to be in the spotlight or network with anyone through Holden."

"I saw a video your sister-in-law or something posted about you confirming you're dating Holden. Why do that if you aren't seeking attention?"

I toss back the rest of my wine. Would one of my brother's wives do that? Yes, probably. Who? Candace most likely. Or maybe her sister, Suzanne. Technically we're related and I could see her doing something like that.

"I haven't seen any video, so I can't comment on what they said. However, I can assure you the last thing I'm seeking is attention. If I was, I wouldn't have been hiding out at my friend's house or avoiding my own store or home when the news hit."

She rests her elbows on the bar and leans back with one of her shoes resting on the rail running along the bottom of the bar. "You claim to not want notoriety, but yet you're dating a celebrity. Seems a little counterintuitive if you ask me. Then there's the fact you sought out my nephew at a wedding. Tell me how that wasn't insinuating yourself into a position to meet his famous father?"

I glance behind me to ensure everyone else is occupied and out of earshot. I will not cause a scene, and I refuse to make a bad impression on the rest of his family. Tori is, apparently, a lost cause. She already thinks the worst of me. I step closer to her.

"I can see how or why you have such a terrible impression of me. You're protecting your brother and nephew, and I can understand and even applaud that. However, I had no idea who Trevor was at the wedding until after. All I knew was he was a kid alone. I have no control over what someone related to me might or might not have said. Yes, I admit I told my mother I am dating Holden. Maybe that wasn't the smartest thing to do. This is what I do know. I care about your brother and Trevor very much. Where is this relationship going? I have no idea. We're getting to know each other and taking one day at a time. There're no guarantees in life, and I doubt anyone goes into a relationship knowing how it will play out. If you have any actual questions to ask me rather than accusations, I'll be happy to answer them. That's the best I can do."

Tori glances over my shoulder just as a warm hand rubs down my back. "Everything all right?"

I smile over my shoulder at Holden. "Just fine."

He glances between me and his sister. "Tor, you're making my guest feel welcome, right?"

"Just looking out for my family. You don't have the best track record when it comes to women."

His body stiffens beside me. I put my arm around him and rub his back. I will not be the reason a fight breaks out between him and his sister.

"Tori's concerned I have ulterior motives for dating you. I think... hope...I've put the worries to rest. But, as I told her, I'm happy to answer any questions."

"For God's sake, Tor."

"What? Like you haven't asked questions of a guy Tess or I dated?"

"That's my job as your big brother, number one. Number two, I didn't accuse them of anything except trying to get in your pants."

She sets her empty bottle on the bar. "Don't much see the difference." She sighs and studies me. "As long as you don't hurt my family, I got no problem with you. Now, since Trev has trounced Tess, I need to go show that little squirt who's boss."

Tori wanders over to the pool table.

Holden lets out a sigh. "Sorry about that. I had no idea she would be so difficult. I've never brought a woman here before or introduced them to my family, so I guess I had no precedence to base my assurances to you that everything would be fine. I'll talk to her."

I grab his arm. "No, you won't. She said her piece and I said mine. She's not going to like me any better if you lecture her or argue with her. Hopefully, she'll come to like me on her own. If we continue dating, that is."

"What's that mean? She chasing you off already?"

"Not at all. I'm simply stating the obvious. Neither one of us has any idea where this will lead. We have a lot of challenges to overcome."

"Like what? I thought we were past the paparazzi thing."

"We are. That incident, anyway. Patty said there haven't been any lurking outside the store. There's still the fact I live in New Hampshire and you live in Texas. You're still a celebrity, which poses its own set of problems. Then there's all the normal growing pains a couple has to go through when they start a relationship."

He slips his arms around my waist and rests his hands against my lower back. "The only thing that matters is our feelings for one another and if we're compatible. The past few days have proven we are. There are solutions to everything else if you try hard enough."

Chapter Thirteen

Holden reclines on the end of my bed, massaging my feet. "You're entirely too good at this. Did you play a masseuse or something in a movie?"

"Nope." He presses his thumb along the arch of my foot.

"Then where did you learn? You're not going to tell me it's a natural ability you have, are you?"

"I dated a massage therapist once."

"Ah, I see." I pull my foot away. "On second thought." I put my foot back in front of him. "I will not let a moment of jealousy deprive me of a great massage."

His lips twist. "Jealousy? Why would you be jealous? I dated her for like a minute and picked up some techniques. I knew the relationship was going nowhere, which is why I never introduced her to Trev or even mentioned her to anyone I care about." He massages the back of my ankle and up my calves.

"Don't worry, the jealousy passed quickly. I'm starting to feel downright thankful to her."

"Then I should keep going?"

"Absolutely."

"To be clear, I only picked up a few massage moves from her. Everything else is my technique alone."

I smirk. "You have a technique?"

He shoots me a mock glare as his hands transform my legs into warm Play-Doh. All tension has drained from my body. He places a soft kiss against my knee.

"I acknowledge you might have some moves."

He places a kiss against the other knee.

I'm leaving in the morning. We haven't made any concrete plans to see one another again. What if the distance proves too great a barrier and we end the relationship? Before I've had a chance to know what it's like to make love to him?

It can't still be considered impulsive anymore, can it?

His hands massage my thigh as his lips caress the back of my knee.

"Sexual compatibility is an important ingredient in a dating relationship. Wouldn't you agree?"

Holden pauses, and his glance meets mine. "You're definitely talking my language here, but I don't want to pressure or rush you. I'm fairly confident we're more than sexually compatible. In fact, I think combustible might be a better term."

"I agree, and I'm really tired of waiting." I run the edge of my foot down his side. "Why don't you grab my purse? I think it's time we put that condom to use."

"No need. I brought my own." He reaches over, opens the nightstand drawer, and takes out a package of condoms.

"When did you put those in there?"

"The day after that night. I wanted to be prepared." He pauses. "Too presumptuous?"

"No, I was just curious when and how you did it."

I untie my robe and let it fall open. His gaze caresses my entire body. The heat and passion burns in his eyes.

"I'm real fond of your desire for baths and wearing robes after." His lips explore my navel.

"I'd like to do some exploring of my own. But you're way overdressed."

His T-shirt goes flying across the room. The slide and snap of leather soon follows when he removes his belt. He stands and shucks his jeans and underwear in seconds. As he toes off his socks, I slip my arms out of the robe and unclasp my bra.

I stand in front of him and let my bra fall to the floor while I shimmy out of my panties. He sucks in a breath. The warmth of its release flows over my shoulder as he kisses my shoulder all the way up to my neck.

His hands span my waist and propel me flush against him. The heat and hard planes of his body act like an aphrodisiac.

I spread my hands over his chest and shoulders learning every ridge and plane.

Holden's mouth captures mine in a searing kiss, which resonates through my core.

"Like I said, combustible." His lips suck on my bottom lip as his hands cup my breasts. "Lie down, Angel. I want to learn every inch of you and what you like."

His hands and mouth do indeed explore every inch of me and somewhere along the way my mind turns to mush and I lose track of time and place.

"Still with me?" His words whisper against the side of my breast.

"Not sure. I think I might have had an out-of-body experience."

He chuckles against my skin. The tear of plastic and shift of the mattress prompt me to drag my eyes open.

Holden is like a blond God rising above me.

I lift my arms and drag him back to me. The weight and warmth of him is a separate pleasure all of its own. I let my kiss do my talking and try to convey all the feelings roaring inside me. They're like a category five hurricane battering my defenses with winds so strong it can crumble the foundation beneath my feet.

I push his shoulders without stopping our kiss. He rolls with me to his back, and I straddle him. Our lips part, and he cups my cheek. I stare into his eyes as I join us together. His hands clutch my hips, and he waits for me to set the pace.

My body feels like a torch set aflame.

Our gazes are as locked as our bodies.

A sheen of perspiration coats his golden skin.

The tingling starts at the base of my spine. My entire body clenches, and waves of pleasure crash over me.

Holden groans low and clamps his hands on my hips.

I collapse, boneless, on top of him.

His arms wrap tight around me. His chest rises and falls rapidly. The thump of his heartbeat echoes against my cheek.

"Combustible might be too tame a word after all." His slow drawl accompanies his hands caressing my back and shoulders.

"Volcano?" My insides certainly feel like lava.

"Mmm…I was thinking more like a supernova."

"Yeah, I think I saw stars at one point."

He chuckles and kisses the top of my head. "Not sure how we can top that, but I'm up for the challenge…in a little while, anyway."

Chapter Fourteen

"Still hiding in the back?" Rebecca, Franny, and Lucinda waltz through the door. Rebecca and Franny smile while Lucinda waves and grins. Is she ever in a bad mood? If she is, I don't think she'd let it show.

I push away from my desk. "Yes, although it's not so much from paparazzi anymore. Except for the occasional lurker, they've disappeared over the past week. It's all the questions my customers have about Holden that have forced me into hiding this time."

Lucinda pouts. "Does that mean we can't ask questions? Because I've been dying to."

Franny rolls her eyes as she tugs off her heavy coat. "She's not kidding. I've done my best to hold her back, but I'm afraid I gave up today. Sorry. I generally hide in the kitchen at the bakery anyway, but after Mitch and I became an item, I didn't venture out front for at least a month to avoid all the questions."

Rebecca plants her butt on the edge of my desk and unbuttons her coat. It falls open to reveal a dark gray wool dress and black knee-high boots. "I've been doling out the little snippets you've told me, but I'm afraid it's not enough anymore. We're in need of a gossip session with you as the chief attraction."

Lucinda wrinkles her nose. "I guess I can behave myself if you really don't want to share, but at least tell me if he's as swoon-worthy of a kisser as he appears to be in the movies."

I try to firm my features into a stern expression but end up smirking instead. "Better."

"Oh, goody." Lucinda holds her hands together in prayer. "Please share."

I clear fabric off the only other chairs in the backroom. "Have a seat. Sorry, but I'm not used to entertaining back here." I glance around the small, cluttered space. "I keep meaning to organize but somehow I always come up with excuses not to."

"I'll help you in exchange for sharing some details." Lucinda folds her pink wool coat over the back of the chair. She perches on the edge of the chair with her hands folded in her lap.

Franny slides into the chair next to her sister. "Olivia is going to be jealous. Someone had to stay and watch the bakery, so we flipped a coin and I won." She glances down at the box in her lap. "I almost forgot." She hands the box to Rebecca, who puts it on my desk. "This is a bribe. Olivia's idea. Your favorite cupcakes."

I grin. "You guys are the best. I'll tell you anything you want to know. Well…within reason."

Rebecca waves a hand. "Don't worry, I'm a firm believer a little mystery is a good thing. We won't ask for measurements or anything."

Lucinda leans forward with a dramatic leer. "Unless you really want to tell us."

"All I'll say on that subject is there are no concerns."

"Let's change the subject or I'll never be able to look at Holden again without blushing." Franny places her hands over her pink cheeks.

"Good idea. What exactly is it you want to know?" I glance at each of them.

Rebecca tilts her head toward me. "Are you exclusive or is this a casual thing?"

"Exclusive. He actually brought it up before I left. I had been wondering how to broach the subject, but he beat me to it, thankfully."

"What did he say?" Rebecca grips the edge of the desk and crosses her ankles. "We want specifics."

We'd been lying in each other's arms after making love for the second time, and he'd run his fingers up and down my arm in a lazy pattern. But I'm not going to share those details.

"He said he wasn't interested in dating anyone else and wanted to know if I felt the same. I, of course, said yes."

Lucinda leans forward. "Why 'of course'? Are you in love with him?"

I open my mouth and close it. Am I in love with Holden?

"I...I'm not sure yet. I mean, I have powerful feelings for him."

"That's been rather clear from the beginning." Rebecca laughs. "The sparks flew anytime you were anywhere near one another. I just wasn't sure if you were going come to blows or hop into bed. Glad to see it's the latter."

"Hilarious. He sure managed to rub me the wrong way. Although to be fair, I may have had some lingering resentment clouding my judgment where he was concerned." I glance at each of them. "Holden and I actually met years ago when I was working as a glorified intern for a fashion designer in Manhattan. I was fresh out of college and so very naïve. Hindsight is twenty-twenty, you know?"

They're all staring at me with eager expressions like they can't wait to hear what I'll say next. "Anyway, I stepped into the elevator, and there he was, the hot, new celebrity featured on the billboard in Times Square. I'd met a few celebrities before so it wasn't like I was starstruck or anything, but it was like my whole body became like a glass of just-poured champagne—effervescent."

Lucinda sucks in a breath and puts her hand over her chest. "Love at first sight."

"I don't know about love, but there was a definite attraction. He flirted, and I flirted back. I could smell the alcohol on his breath when he rested his arm over my head and leaned close, so I knew he wasn't sober. Any thought about that went right out of my head when he kissed me. Then the elevator dinged, the doors opened, and his entourage dragged him away. I never saw him again until he walked into my shop and didn't recognize me. I assumed he'd been too drunk, too uninterested, and our kiss meant nothing to him. Honestly, I was embarrassed I had held on to the memory for so long."

"What did he say when you reminded him?" Lucinda frowns. "You did tell him?"

"Actually, no, I had no intention of dragging that particular piece of information into the light of day. I intended to take it to my grave."

"Oh my gosh! I knew I heard this story before. At least a similar version." Franny slaps the arms of the chair and grins.

"What do you mean?"

"Holden told Mitch a story about the Angel in the elevator once. He said he wasn't sure if he dreamed you or not. He went back the next day searching for you. I'd forgotten all about it until you started telling your story. It is you, isn't it?" She gets a horrified expression on her face and fingers her necklace. "Please tell me it's you and I haven't just swallowed my whole foot and leg, too."

"Yes, it's me. He remembered that night he came to your house to talk to me. I didn't have a drop of makeup on and my hair was up in a messy bun. I guess I looked similar enough to back then to trigger his memory."

Franny sags against the chair. "Thank goodness."

"That is so romantic!" Lucinda clasps both hands over her chest.

Rebecca lightly shoves my shoulder. "I can't believe you kept that a secret all this time."

"Look who's talking. I recall a certain someone kept a heck of a lot of secrets of their own."

She wobbles her head back and forth. "Point taken."

Lucinda claps her hands together. "Tell us more. When are you going to see him again?"

"Actually, we've been trying to figure that out. He's got commitments he can't get out of, and I can't leave the store again so soon. All the newfound popularity has kept the shop pretty busy. I have a lot of brides making appointments. There was an enormous surge after Franny and Mitch's wedding, and now it's happening again. I think a few of them have hopes of running into Mitch or Holden here at the shop. I can't complain, though. Sales are way up."

"When Mitch first came back to town, The Sweet Spot gained a lot of new customers—most of them female. He'd stop in almost every morning and the lines would form in anticipation. I was thankful for the added business, too, even when I wasn't too happy with him."

I smile at Franny. "How do you handle all the attention being married to a celebrity? Is it hard?"

"It was a major hurtle for me because I'm so shy and my insecurities took over. But it has gotten easier, and Mitch isn't in the spotlight much. As a director, his face isn't on the big screen or in advertisements. I'm sorry, but I think it's quite different for Holden."

"I'm not married to a celebrity, but most relationships have to be built on trust and love. If you have enough of both, then nothing else matters." Rebecca shrugs. "Of course, I didn't believe either was possible, and Ian had his hands full convincing me otherwise."

"That's for sure. I felt sorry for Ian." Franny chuckles. "He would chase after you at every business meeting."

I smirk at Rebecca. "It was fun to watch, though."

Rebecca rolls her eyes. "I'm so glad I was here for your amusement."

"Oh, come on, it was very clear—to us, anyway—that you were not immune to his charms."

She sends me a mock glare. "Fine, but could someone explain to me how I became the subject of this conversation? We were talking about your relationship with Holden."

"The way things are going, I doubt I'll see him until after the holidays. I've already told my family I won't be going home to Chicago for Christmas this year. My mother has been trying to guilt me into going with her typical manipulations. She believes the silent treatment doesn't extend to texts. So she won't call me to show her displeasure, but she sends me random texts about how she's getting older and won't always be around. Sometimes she switches to my grandmother or father. This morning it was a text saying my nieces and nephews won't even recognize me by the time I get around to visiting again." I shake my head. "They all just saw me for Thanksgiving. She acts like it's been years."

Rebecca folds her arms over her chest. "If she misses you so much, why can't she come visit you for a change? Didn't you say your family has never been here?"

"My family thinks I've moved to the middle of the woods. I doubt very much they'll ever set foot in Granite Cove. If it's not a city, they don't think it's worth their time."

"But you're their daughter. You should be worth their time no matter where you live."

I give Rebecca a small smile. "Not all families are close."

"Well, you're all part of my family now, and since it's Mitch's and my first Christmas together as a married couple, we've decided to host a small Christmas Eve party and you're all invited. Please say you'll come."

Lucinda stretches over and squeezes her sister's hand. "You know I'll be there."

"I have to check with Ian. His huge family has multiple traditions. I know we're all going to the farm on Christmas Day, but I don't think we have anything planned for Christmas Eve." She frowns. "Is this just for couples?"

Franny shakes her head. "Oh no, it's for all of you. Drew and Rachelle are absolutely invited. Olivia and Luke are bringing the boys so Drew will have someone to play with."

Rebecca smiles. "Drew will be thrilled."

Holden hasn't mentioned the holidays. I assume he and Trevor will spend them with his family. I guess it's too early in our relationship to expect to be included in family celebrations.

"I'll be there, too. Tell me what I can bring."

Franny holds up her hands. "Not a thing. I've got it all planned out. I just want you to all come and have fun."

I better finish my Christmas shopping for Trevor and Holden so I can wrap and ship their gifts to Texas. A pang hits the center of my chest. The brightness of the holidays just dimmed.

Chapter Fifteen

The window displays are missing something. The puffy, fake snow on the floor could be deeper, but that's not the problem. There are no missing or broken bulbs in the strands of white lights edging the two display areas. The fake wrapped presents in ivory and gold are a suitable backdrop without detracting from my product. The emerald-green dress on one side and the red jumpsuit on the other both provide a color pop and are the focus of the displays like I intended. The two pieces are both excellent choices for a holiday party. Perhaps it's the mannequins? I could change the hairstyles or maybe just add accessories.

An older man with silver hair and glasses shuffles into the store. His wooden cane taps against the floor. He must be in his late seventies or early eighties judging by the number of wrinkles fanning out from his eyes and the hunched set of his shoulders. Is he here to rent a tuxedo for a special event? Maybe his granddaughter is getting married. Or maybe he's getting married. I shouldn't jump to conclusions.

"Hello. Welcome to Dress to Impress. How can I help you today?"

"You can get your sweet little self over here and give me a kiss." His voice is gravely with age and probably years of smoking.

I rear my head back. It's not the first time I've been propositioned, but it is by a man old enough to be my grandfather.

"Um...sir, that's not appropriate." With my luck, he's the grandfather of one of my brides, so I don't want to cause a big fuss. What if he's senile and confused?

A familiar warm chuckle sends a tingle down my spine. *No, it couldn't be!* I peer closer.

The side of the man's mouth inches up into a smirk.

"Holden?"

"Hi, Angel. I'm still waiting for my kiss." He straightens his back and opens his arms with the cane he was leaning so heavily on dangling from his arm. His soft drawl is back.

I stride across the floor and leap into his arms.

He wraps his arms around me and swings me off the floor.

Tears fill my eyes. *God, have I missed him!* The daily calls and multiple texts aren't enough. I press my cheek to his and fold my arms around his neck. "This is a delightful surprise."

"It feels good to have you back in my arms." He tilts his nose against my neck and breathes deep. "I missed your smell."

I laugh. "I hope it's a pleasant smell."

"It is. Like sitting on the ranch porch after a good rain when everything is fresh and sparkles in the sun."

"In that case, sniff away."

He laughs and lifts his head. "I missed you."

"I missed you, too, but it's a little weird hearing your voice come out of this old man."

He grins and kisses me.

The fake moustache is scratchy, but I don't care because it's Holden's lips on mine.

He sets me on my feet but keeps his arms around my waist. The cane bounces against the back of my leg.

"I wanted to surprise you but thought it better if I came to your store incognito."

"Mission accomplished on both counts. I think you'd fool even Lily and Bo in that getup."

"I've fooled them a few times over the years. Mom usually figures it out first and will play along for a bit."

"Let me just close up and we can go to my place." I peek behind him out the front of the store. "Is Trevor with you? You didn't leave him in Texas, did you?"

"No, he would've found his way here on his own if I tried that. I think he misses you almost as much as I do."

"Then where is he? You left him in the car?"

"He's with Mitch and Franny. I promised him we would pick him up on the way to the cabin."

"You rented the cabin again?"

"Bought a different one. It should take the press awhile before they track down I'm the buyer, and this one has more privacy and it's bigger. I figured we'd be here often enough. Might as well have a place to stay."

I grin and hug him close.

"We better get out of here before someone spots us and spreads a rumor about you cheating on me with an old man."

I swat him lightly on the shoulder. "Don't joke about that. They'll label me a gold digger, grave robber, or some other horrible nonsense."

"Okay. What do you need to do?"

"Lock the front door and flip the sign to closed. I'll cash out the register and close up. We'll go out the back to my car." I spin back toward him. "Wait, how did you get here? Do you have a car?"

"Nope, we can take yours. Mitch dropped me off."

I shake my head. "I can't believe Franny didn't tell me. How long have you been planning this?"

"Don't be mad at her. I swore her to silence and only let Mitch tell her a couple of days ago after I had everything worked out. Mitch knew a little longer because he figured into my plans."

So she didn't know when she was here a few days ago with Lucinda and Rebecca. "I'm not mad. I'm thrilled you and Trevor are here. How long can you stay?"

"Trev's out of school until after the holidays, and he's really looking forward to a white Christmas. If it's okay with you, I thought we'd spend it here in Granite Cove with you—unless you have other plans. You didn't change your mind about going to Chicago, did you?"

Someone just turned the dial on my internal Christmas light switch to maximum illumination.

"Nope, I'm all yours. This is the best Christmas present!"

"Oh, good, I guess I can send your other gifts back." He walks over to the door and locks it.

I pick up a pad of paper next to the register and throw it at him. It misses him by a mile.

He laughs and picks it up. "I guess I need to teach you how to throw. On second thought, maybe not."

I gasp. "I mailed your presents to Texas!"

Dang it! Now I'll have nothing to give them. I'll have to go shopping and get them something else for Christmas Day.

"You mean those packages Franny offered to handle for you?"

I sag against the register.

"I never knew she could be so sneaky."

Holden laughs. "She finds it romantic."

"I guess I'll have to thank her instead of scold her."

He walks behind me, wraps his arms around my waist, and rests his chin on my shoulder. "Why don't you show me your backroom?"

"Mr. Fox, are you propositioning me again?"

"Yep."

I glance down at his age spot–speckled arm and laugh. "You have to remove the disguise first. I don't think I'll be able to keep a straight face otherwise."

"It took me hours to put on this getup, and it'll take a while to remove, too. Sure you can't just close your eyes?"

"Holden!"

"Just a thought." He sighs. "I guess I'll have to wait until tonight when we're at the cabin and Trev is asleep."

"Don't sound so forlorn. Waiting builds sexual tension."

He snorts. "Not for the guy. It just gives us a case of blue balls."

I frown and twist in his arms. "We could stop at my place first."

He drops his forehead to mine. "Don't mind me. A few more hours is better than the days I've waited to touch you again."

"Then let's get out of here. Time will go faster now that we're together."

Chapter Sixteen

Gold ribbons twine among the branches. Tiny white lights twinkle amidst the green needles. Ornaments perch or dangle from almost every available spot.

"I don't think that Christmas tree would fit in my apartment, let alone through the door. It would take up my entire living room. How on earth did you get it in here?" It's easily twice my height and ten times my width. "It's absolutely gorgeous, though."

Franny laughs. "Mitch had to hire someone to set it up. It was a whole production."

"I entirely underestimated my tree cutting and transporting abilities when Franny and I went Christmas tree shopping." Mitch puts his arm around his wife.

"It might've had something to do with the size of tree you picked out." Holden tips his head back and stares at the top.

Mitch scratches his chin. "Yeah, Franny had her heart set on this one. She wanted a large tree for the Christmas Eve party. Her and Lucinda poured over decorations and themes." He kisses the top of her head when she grins up at him. "She was right, though. It looks perfect in the corner. We can see it lit up all the way down at the lake."

With the size of the tree and the windows on either side of it, I bet anyone on the islands across the way can see the tree, too. At least the ones who live year-round on the islands would.

"It is beautiful. I never got around to putting my tree up this year."

"That's because you helped Trev and me with ours at the cabin. It's not too late if you want one for your place, too. We can get another one."

"No, mine is only a small, artificial one. I much prefer the one we picked out with Trevor."

Holden casts a doubtful look my way. "He picked out one of the straggliest trees on the lot."

"It's only missing a few branches on one side and you can't even see the bald spot the way it's tucked into the corner of the cabin between the window and the fireplace." I lean closer to Franny. "I think Trevor picked the tree because he was worried no one else would."

Franny puts her hand over her heart. "That is so sweet."

Holden chuckles. "I don't think many would pick it now the way it's decorated, either."

"Hey!" I swat his arm. "It's a very pretty tree. It's not elegant like this one, but it has its own charm."

"The store was sold out of most of the decorations, so Trev and Kelly got a little creative with decorating."

I shrug. "The only lights we could find were blue, but with all the tinsel Trev added, it's a silver-and-blue-themed tree."

"I do like those white little bows you tied to the branches." Holden mimics tying bows. "And the popcorn string was fun even if we gave up when it was only a few feet long."

Franny gasps. "I always wanted to make one of those growing up, but my mother always said no. It didn't go with whatever theme she had decided on that year." She glances up at Mitch. "I wish I'd remembered that. We could've done one."

"There's always next year. I do have to agree with Holden. It is a lot of work. Of course, he and Trevor kept eating the popcorn, too."

"What are the four of you giggling about?" Rebecca glances at each one of us.

"Men don't giggle, sweetheart." Ian puts his arm around her shoulders.

Both Mitch and Holden nod.

Rebecca rolls her eyes. "Fine, are 'laugh' or 'chuckle' permissible for your manly sensibilities?"

Ian purses his lips and tilts his head back. "Both of those terms are acceptable."

"We were just admiring the tree and then talking about the tree Trevor picked out for the cabin." I rest my head on Holden's shoulder. "Did you guys put up a Christmas tree?"

"Yes." Rebecca stares at the floor.

Ian snorts. "It was quite the debate."

She sighs. "It's our first Christmas together, so we're still learning to merge our traditions. Ian has always had an actual tree. In fact, his entire family only have real trees. It's a thing, apparently."

"Rebecca, on the other hand, always had artificial trees. She thought it wasn't environmentally friendly to have a real Christmas tree." Ian takes a sip of his drink and smiles. "We compromised and bought a tree with the root ball still intact, and we're going to plant it in the yard after Christmas. It should be fun trying to dig a hole in frozen ground."

Rebecca lifts her glass of wine with a smile. "It'll give you a chance to show off those muscles of yours." She blows Ian a kiss. "Besides, Drew already picked out the spot, and he wants to decorate it next year and every year after."

"If we do this every year, we're going to have our own Christmas tree farm in our yard." Ian winks at Rebecca and takes another sip of his drink.

"True, but each tree will have precious memories attached to it." Rebecca points her finger at me. "Before I forget, Drew really wants to have a playdate, or whatever you want to call it, with Trevor." She glances between Holden and me. "How long is Trevor going to be in Granite Cove?"

I turn my head to Holden. It's his decision.

Holden rubs my hip. "We'll be here until after the New Year, then Trev has to get back to Texas for school. We can schedule something before then. I know he'd love it, too."

Olivia peeks her head between Rebecca and me. "My boys will want in on that action, too. Speaking of which, we've gotta run. We have to get them over to Ryan's parents' house."

"Are you still celebrating the holidays with them?" Franny frowns as she steps forward and clasps Olivia's hands. "I thought you were going to stop running from house to house trying to please everyone all the time."

Olivia squeezes Franny's hands. "I am and I have. We're only dropping Timmy and Tommy off. Ryan will bring them back before noon tomorrow."

Luke rubs Olivia shoulders from behind. "Don't worry, she's learned to say no."

"It's still a learning process, but Ryan and I are both in agreement it doesn't help the boys any if we run them ragged by dragging them from one celebration to the next. Which is why we're taking turns or combining each of the holidays this year. And we've really gotta go." Olivia kisses Franny's cheek. "Thanks so much for having us. It's been a wonderful Christmas Eve."

"You could come back after you drop the boys off." Franny glances over her shoulder at Mitch. "We're going to play Christmas games later on."

Olivia glances up at Luke. "What do you think?"

Luke chuckles. "I think you're vastly underestimating the time it takes to drive back and forth, and the actual handoff of the boys and all their stuff."

Olivia pouts. "You're probably right."

Luke leans down to whisper in her ear. "Besides, I'm looking forward to having you all to myself tonight."

Olivia's face perks up, and she grins. "On second thought, I don't think we'll be able to make it back."

We all laugh, and Olivia, Luke, and the boys make the rounds saying their goodbyes. Lucinda and Franny's parents leave as well. Franny and Mitch escort everyone out while the rest of us sit on the couches by the fireplace.

Lucinda plops down next me with a sigh and leans her head on the back of the couch.

"Everything okay?"

She pries one eye open and peeks at me. "Yes, my mother is just exhausting. I made the mistake of telling her I intend to become a wedding planner instead of going back to practicing law, and she acts like I've told her I'm going to commit a felony or something."

"Ah, I see. My family never understood my career choices, either. My father and brothers are all doctors. My mother worked in human resources at the hospital before she retired. I'm the odd one out."

"Do you think they'll ever stop trying to fit us into whatever hole they've imagined us into?"

"My family? I'd have to say that's a hard no. For yours? I don't know them well, but from what I've seen? I wouldn't hold your breath."

She raises her head. "Hell would probably freeze over first. I need wine."

"Got you covered." Mitch hands her a glass. "Franny sent me with it. She's in the kitchen bringing more food."

I glance around at the array of hors d'oeuvres on the giant, square coffee table between the pair of couches. "More food?"

Mitch puts his hands in his front pockets and frowns. "I know. I tried to tell her she didn't need to prepare so much. I even made the mistake of suggesting we hire a caterer. She glared at me like I suggested we serve everyone mud and didn't speak to me for two hours."

Lucinda winces. "Blame our mother for that one." She takes a healthy swallow of wine.

"Yeah, I realized that eventually. Wish I remembered before I opened my mouth."

"If Mother attends the party, I doubt Franny will ever hire a caterer."

"On the contrary, if we ever have a large party, I will definitely hire a caterer." Franny hands Mitch two platters covered in desserts. She consolidates the remaining appetizers and creates space for the new platters. "For small gatherings like this, I'll probably still want to do most of it myself. Although it's no longer to prove a point to my mother. It's because I actually enjoy it."

She takes the platters from Mitch and places them on the table. "And because on her way out, Mother asked me who my caterer was because she wanted to hire them for her next party. I politely said that wasn't a possibility because I did everything myself. She was satisfactorily speechless."

Lucinda holds up her hand, and Franny high fives her. "Way to go, Sis. You showed her." Lucinda leans closer to me. "Our mother has always been less than supportive about Franny owning a bakery."

"How can she resist your creations? I'm addicted." I lean forward and snatch a little cheesecake.

"Speaking from personal experience, never get between Kelly and your desserts." Holden pops a cream puff into his mouth.

I wrinkle my nose at him.

"Mother has never set foot in my bakery. She's stopped trying to get me to change careers, but that's probably only because she's focused on Luce."

"I've gained even more respect for you, Franny. I don't know how you've done it all these years." Lucinda ponders the tray of desserts before picking up a piece of baklava. "I fantasized about taping her mouth shut the entire time she lectured me."

Franny cups her hand over her mouth. "I've imagined worse."

"How about we do something more pleasant than discuss your mother?" Mitch rubs his hands together. "Time for games?"

"Good idea." Franny points to a door on the far wall. "The boxes are in that closet."

While Mitch heads to the closet, Franny smiles and sits in the chair. "I downloaded all these Christmas games and wrapped individual presents to hand out to the winners. It was so much fun." She hops back up. "Trevor, Drew, it's time for games!"

The boys lift their heads from the LEGO spaceship they've been working on. Neither of them move.

"I happen to know there are more LEGO hiding in a package or two." Mitch puts down a giant box overflowing with wrapped gifts.

Both boys jump up and come over to the couches.

Chapter Seventeen

Trevor peers at his rock specimen and types on his laptop. He measures the rock and even examines it under a magnifying glass. I guess the assortment of rocks I got him as one of his gifts is a hit. I knew he was a rock collector, but what I didn't know is he keeps a detailed database on each rock in his laptop.

Waldo sleeps on the floor next to Trevor. I think my dog might have defected over to him. The fire crackles beyond him in the stone fireplace. Holden's new cabin is about three times the size of the one he rented over the summer. Giant wood beams span the ceiling of the great room. A wall of glass showcases the frozen lake view.

I tug the soft, fake fur blanket under my chin.

"Cold?" Holden tucks the blanket around my legs and feet resting in his lap. "I can add more wood to the fire."

"No, I'm good. In fact, this entire day has been perfect."

We woke up to big, fat snowflakes drifting from the sky as the sun rose over the lake. A truly white Christmas morning. Trevor was ecstatic. I think it ranked right up there with opening presents.

"I have to agree. Today has been pretty perfect." He slips his hands under the blanket and rubs my feet.

He stares at Trevor with a slight smile on his face. His blond hair hangs over his forehead. He's past due for a trim. Holden catches me staring at him and grins.

My heart trips in my chest like I've tripped over my own feet walking down a hill.

I'm in love with him—completely, madly in love with Holden Fox.

"What's wrong?" His eyebrows lower, and he frowns.

"Nothing." I shake my head. "Nothing is wrong."

"You sure?"

"Like I said, it's a perfect day."

"That expression looked more like you had indigestion or something. Dinner not sitting well?"

I briefly close my eyes. Great, I realize I'm in love with him and he thinks I'm sick to my stomach. "Dinner was perfect, too. You did an excellent job with the prime rib and potatoes."

"I know how to cook a steak."

"Yes, you can officially handle all cooking duties from now on."

"I can get behind that as long as you take care of the baking. That cake thingy was good. I might have another piece soon."

"Tiramisu trifle. Franny actually gave me the recipe and detailed instructions. It was surprisingly easy. I'll add to my short list of things I can make for guests."

"I wouldn't say it's a short list. Those waffles you made this morning with the strawberries and whipped cream were delicious."

"Mmm...my repertoire is expanding."

"You're not sad you didn't go to Chicago for Christmas?"

"No, not at all. Are you sad you didn't stay in Texas?"

"Not a bit. I miss my family. The only thing that could make this day more perfect is to have them here, but we'll see them soon enough."

True, Trevor had to go back to school so they would be leaving in a little over a week. Tears smart at my eyes. I swallow hard and blink. I still have over a week left with them, and I'm not going to worry about missing them while they're still here with me.

"How did the call with your family go?"

I wiggle down and rest my head on the arm of the couch. "About as expected. My mother thought I was pulling one of my impulsive Kelly Anne moments as she calls them by not coming home for Christmas. I guess she thought I would still show up and wasn't happy when I didn't."

She had gotten emotional and handed the phone off to my father, who had grumbled about the weather and then wished me a merry Christmas.

"I happen to like your impulsivity."

"You do, do you?"

Holden glances at Trevor and then scoots across the couch closer to me. I sit up a little and make room.

He leans close to my cheek. "Mmm hmm, like the time you surprised me wearing light blue lingerie."

"How do you know I didn't plan that out?"

"Did you?"

"No." I had found the outfit stuffed way at the back of my drawer with the tags still on. Holden had been waiting for me in my living room while I packed an overnight bag. I'd slipped on the lingerie and waltzed out into the living room. He'd been very appreciative.

Holden's finger traces the outer shell of my ear. His breath tickles the hairs on the back of my neck. "Then there was that time you slipped into my morning shower with me."

I glance over at Trevor to make sure he's still engrossed with his rocks.

"Then there was just this morning when you ran outside in nothing but my shirt to grab your bag out of your car. That sight is burned into my memory. Especially when you bent over to reach into the back seat."

I shiver dramatically. "Probably not the smartest thing I've done. It was freezing."

He wraps an arm around my back and legs and lifts me so I'm sitting in his lap. "You should've told me and I would've gotten it for you. I did an excellent job of warming you up after, didn't I?"

"Yes, you get a gold star."

"Do I need to go to my room?" Trevor stares at us with a smirk on his face.

I try to scramble off Holden's lap, but he holds me close.

"Kelly was cold. I'm warming her up."

"Uh huh. I've had health class, Dad."

A YEARING DILEMMA

My face heats, and I shove out of Holden's arms.

He laughs and keeps his arm around me while I sit primly next to him with the blanket wrapped around me.

Trevor stands. "I actually need to go to my room. I want to get the rock book Grandma and Grandpa sent me." He checks his phone. "I'd say you have a good fifteen minutes to get any mushy stuff out of your system before I return."

I drop my head and groan while Holden laughs out load. "I think you've destroyed any chance of that, kid."

"Stop laughing! It's mortifying. We have to be more careful when Trevor's around."

"My son is exceedingly smart. He grew up on a ranch and knows all about the birds and bees."

"That doesn't mean we can't set an example and practice a little restraint in his presence. Do you like to watch your parents get affectionate in front of you?"

He grimaces. "Please don't put that image in my head."

"See?"

He chuckles and hugs me to his chest. "His parents, huh?"

"I didn't mean...I'm not...I just meant—"

"Relax, Angel, I know what you meant. I like that you're always looking out for him, and I like the thought of you as his mother, too."

Tears fill my eyes and overflow. I hiccup back the sob trying to escape.

Holden gathers me in his arms. "Don't cry. What did I say? If it's too soon—"

I shake my head violently.

"Not too soon?"

I grip his sweater and shake my head again. "I love him. I love you."

He lifts my chin, and I raise my gaze to meet his.

"I love you, too, Angel. So much."

His lips brush mine, and I sigh into his kiss. He wipes the tears from my face with his hands and continues kissing me.

I tuck my head between his neck and shoulder. His sweater is almost as soft as the blanket, and I burrow in like a bear cub preparing for winter. He loves me.

He rests his cheek on top of my head. "I'm pretty sure I fell in love with you in that elevator years ago. But I know I fell in love with you all over again that first day in Texas when we went riding. You stared all around you talking about how beautiful it was, but all I could see was how beautiful you are and how right it felt to have you there. I vowed then I was going to make you mine."

I lift my head and gape at him. "Why didn't you tell me?"

"Because I didn't want to scare you off and I was waiting for some sign from you that you felt the same way."

"I do." I tuck my head back. Would he have scared me away? Maybe. I wasn't sure of my feelings then. I might have felt it was too soon.

"Glad you two have finally got that settled." Trevor walks into the room and sits back down with his presents.

"Didn't I teach you not to eavesdrop?"

Trevor glances at his father. "No. You always taught me to listen to my surroundings before I act."

"Not the same thing, Trev."

"What's the difference?"

I bite my lip to hide my smile.

Holden frowns at Trevor. "There's a difference. I just can't think of an accurate explanation at the moment." He glances at me. "The kid is smarter than me."

"Don't feel bad. I think he's smarter than most."

Chapter Eighteen

"Surprise!" My mother and father stand outside my front door.

Am I hallucinating? Dreaming? I pinch my arm. Nope, they're still standing there.

"Aren't you going to invite us in?" Mom frowns and wiggles her eyebrows.

"Of course, sorry." I step back, and they march past me. I search behind them to make sure I'm not being invaded by the rest of my family.

Waldo whines next to me. I pat the top of his head. "It's okay, boy. Go lie down in your bed."

Holden walks out of the bathroom and stops. His gaze goes from them to me and back again. He smiles and holds out his hand. "You must be Kelly's parents. I'm Holden Fox."

"How do you know they're my parents?"

"Kelly Anne! What has gotten into you? Have you forgotten all your manners?"

"You've shocked them out of me, Mom. What are you doing in Granite Cove? Why didn't you call me and let me know you were coming? I would've picked you up at the airport."

"We wanted to surprise you." She tugs off her gloves and coat.

I take them and my father's as well and hang them up on the tree stand by the door.

"Can I get you anything? A drink?" I could sure use one. I glance at the clock on the stove in the kitchen. It's after noon.

"No, thank you." She glances around the small room and sits on the couch. She pats the seat next to her. "Come sit and tell me all about yourself, Holden."

Wine isn't going to cut it. I should start on the hard stuff. Shame I didn't know they were coming. I would've stocked up.

Dad walks around the room—which takes about ten seconds. "Where's the closest hospital?"

"About ten minutes. There's one in town." Is he going to see if they'll give him some patients to operate on while he's here?

"Sit down, Tom. You're here to visit our daughter, see where she lives, and meet the young man she's dating."

My father obeys, and I sit on the other side of Holden. He squeezes my hand, and I let out a slow breath. Everything will be fine. He loves me. Nothing they say or do will scare him away.

I hope.

"Holden, I'm told you're an actor. Is that lucrative enough to earn a living?"

Oh, good Lord! I drop my head onto my hand. Only my mother would ask one of the biggest movie stars on the planet if he earns enough to make a living.

"I do all right." Holden puts his arm around my shoulders.

"Mom, please."

"What? The man's dating my daughter. I think it's a perfectly legitimate question." She smiles at Holden. "You don't mind, do you?"

He rubs my shoulder. "Not at all. Ask away."

"You have a son, don't you? Where is he?" She searches the room as if Trevor will suddenly pop up from behind the couch or something.

"Trevor. He's with a few friends. We'll pick him up before dinner." He smiles at my parents. "I hope you'll let me take you out for dinner tonight. There are a few great restaurants in town."

"That would be lovely." She turns to look at my father. "Wouldn't it, Tom?"

"Yes, of course. The inn we're staying at said they have a nice restaurant on the premises. What was the name of it, Ci Ci?"

"White Birch Inn. The room was very spacious and nicely appointed. I was pleasantly surprised when we checked in."

Well, at least that answers the question of where they're staying. It's not like I have a guestroom prepared for them.

"I haven't eaten there yet, but I've heard it's good. Kelly, have you eaten there?"

"Hmm? Oh, yes, I have. It's great." I twist my head and stare at Holden's profile. "Is that a good idea? Going out to eat? Maybe we should eat in. I'll cook something."

Holden glances at me and smiles reassuringly. "It'll be fine. We'll eat out."

Will it, though? What if some paparazzi are still lurking around town? It could become a media frenzy or something. We've been careful to avoid public places as much as possible during their stay. When we have gone out in public, Holden will don some sort of disguise so only a die-hard fan would recognize him.

My mother leans forward to stare at me. "Is there some reason you don't want to eat dinner with us?"

"No, it's just that Holden draws a crowd and the media circus has finally dissipated. I don't want to set it off again."

"I hardly see how going out to dinner can cause a stir. It's settled. I'll call and make reservations." She stands. "Tom, get to know your daughter's beau." She retrieves her phone from her purse and walks over to the door.

My father clears his throat and shifts in his chair. "Holden, what does your family do? Are they actors, too?"

"No, ranching."

"Right. You're from Texas, aren't you? I've been to Houston for a medical conference. Is that close to your ranch?"

"It's a couple hours away."

"All set." Mom pats the top of Dad's chair as she walks by, and he leans back with a sigh.

Dad has difficulty with conversation when the subject isn't medical.

Mom sits and crosses her legs. "Tell me about your family, Holden. Any siblings?"

* * *

"What a lovely thing to say, thank you." Mom places her hand on Ms. Callaway's forearm.

I hang back and let them finish their conversation. The inn manager spots me when she turns away from my mother and waves. She's one of my best repeat customers. She always likes to stop in the shop when I get new inventory.

"Kelly Anne, what are you doing loitering by that fern? Come in here." Mom waves me over from the doorway to her room.

"I didn't want to interrupt your conversation with Ms. Callaway. Are you and Dad all packed?" Their flight back to Chicago leaves this afternoon. I think I'm actually a little sad to see them go. The past two days have been surprisingly pleasant.

"What a lovely woman. Did you hear what she said?"

"No." I glance around the room. There's a green bedspread with gold scrollwork covering the king-size bed on the far side of the room. A seating area flanks the fireplace. A door leading to the bathroom stands ajar. "Where's Dad?"

"He went to fill the rental car up with gas. He'll be back in a few minutes. Come in. Sit down."

I sit in one of the chairs and gaze out the window. The snow-covered lake fills the view. "This is a nice room."

"It is, isn't it? I told Ms. Callaway we'd be back even before she told me how much she loves your store and she can see where you get your marvelous sense of style." She fluffs her hair. "From me, of course. Isn't that sweet?"

"It is. She's one of my best customers."

I gave my parents a tour of the shop yesterday. Mom had a ton of questions while Dad gazed around silently.

"I'll have to bring a bigger suitcase next time so I can buy more of your merchandise."

She purchased two outfits and a scarf yesterday.

"Does this mean you're going to stop asking me when I'm going to sell the store and move back to Chicago?"

Mom frowns and sits on the edge of the chair next to me. "Kelly Anne, I realize I might have been overzealous in my efforts to get you to come home. You're my only daughter and I miss you. I like my family close."

"I can understand that, but it's always felt like you don't appreciate what I do or place value on it."

"Oh no." She grabs my hand. "That couldn't be farther from the truth. I guess I don't always express it very well, but I'm so proud of you and all you've accomplished. I envy you, in fact. I never would've had the bravery to move away from my family and start my own business. You've always been the fearless one in the family. I never stand up to my mother. I know she can be difficult. That's going to change."

Fearless? Me?

"From the shocked expression on your face, I see I haven't shared that with you often enough. For that, I'm sorry. Never doubt my love for you."

"I love you, too, Mom. This means a lot, thank you. I'm really glad you decided to come for a visit."

"Me too, and it's way overdue. Who knows? If you decide to stay in Granite Cove, maybe your father and I should get a place here, too, to visit."

"If I decide to stay? I thought you were going to stop trying to convince me to move back to Chicago?"

"Not Chicago. I meant Texas or Los Angeles. Where does Holden live most of the time? Don't actors have to live in California for work?"

"He has a place there, but he spends most of his time in Texas."

"Do they mob him there like they did at dinner the other night?"

It was hardly a mob. A dozen or so fans approached him throughout the meal for pictures and autographs.

"I don't think so. Not in Texas. He grew up there. They're used to him, and it's a small town—even smaller than Granite Cove."

Her eyes get wide. "What will you do with your store if things progress with Holden? I can see the way he looks at you. That man is in love with you."

"We haven't talked about that far in the future yet. I don't know."

Will Holden expect me to leave Granite Cove and move to Texas? He bought the new place here, but Trevor's school is in Texas.

"That sounds like a conversation you need to have with him sooner rather than later."

"I suppose you're right."

Dad walks in. "Ready to go?"

"Yes, all right, don't walk us out because I'll start crying." She hugs me tight and pecks me on the cheek. "I'll do better."

"Me too, Mom."

Dad kisses me on the cheek, and I watch them walk out the door. I sniffle a little and wander over to the window. I've spent years distancing myself from my family because I thought they didn't understand me or even like me very much. I wish we'd been honest and open with each other years ago.

I wipe the stray tear from my cheek. What matters is I don't feel like the disappointment of the family anymore, and I can understand and empathize a bit more with my mother and her motives.

We're all a product of our upbringing to a certain extent. We have to choose who we want to be when we're adults and let our past go.

I guess that's what I've been doing all along—choosing who I want to be.

I want to be with Holden and Trevor, but how will it work? My life is here in Granite Cove, and theirs are in Texas.

Am I willing to sell my store and start over in Texas?

If it means being with Holden and Trevor, yes.

Now the question is do I wait until he asks or do I ask him?

Chapter Nineteen

My fingers play with the blond hairs on Holden's chest as I lie in his arms. Lights pan across the top of the wall from between the closed curtains. A car must be driving into the parking lot. I need heavier curtains in my bedroom.

They fly home to Texas tomorrow. I've already booked my flight to visit them in two weeks, but it seems so far away. We've spent every day together for weeks now. The thought of going back to solitary meals and sleeping alone while missing them is a heavy ache in my chest.

Holden's phone vibrates on my nightstand. "It might be Trev." He reaches over and picks it up. His frown deepens as he reads the text.

I sit up and drag the sheet with me. "Is it Trevor? What's wrong?" He's sleeping over Olivia's house tonight with the twins. Could he have fallen, gotten hurt somehow?

Holden shakes his head and puts his hand on my thigh. "It's not Trevor. He's fine."

"Then what is it? Your parents? Sisters? Tell me."

"Everyone is fine. It's nothing. It was just my publicist."

"And? Don't tell me it's nothing. I saw your face."

"It *is* nothing." He lies back down and opens his arms. "Let's focus on what matters. It's our last night together for two weeks. I don't want to waste it on nonsense."

I lie back on his chest. The beeping of a truck backing up on the road in front of my building echoes in the night. It's probably a snowplow.

What would his publicist text him about? Did someone snap another picture of us? Of him and someone else?

I chew on my bottom lip. "If you just tell me what it's about, I'll be able to stop thinking the worst."

"Samantha was on a talk show and made a comment. It's nothing. It doesn't matter."

I sit up. "What did she say?"

He folds his arms over his head. "Why do you want to discuss this now?"

"Because my mind will imagine all sorts of horrible things if you don't tell me. It's better to know than be left in the dark. I could probably find out what she said online. I'm sure plenty of people will tell me over the next few days, too." I glance at my phone on the charging stand.

"Fine. She said some stuff about you. Said a concerned person close to you told her you have a checkered past riddled with scandals. She made a tearful act about how worried she is to have her son around someone like this."

I wrap my arms around my legs as tears fill my eyes.

"See!" He throws his hands in the air. "Why didn't you just let it go? Now you're upset. It means nothing. It's just another of her pack of lies to get attention. You can't let it bother you."

"How am I supposed to not be upset by her hateful attack on me? How can you dismiss it so easily?"

"Because I don't care what she says. Every word that comes out of her mouth is a lie."

"Why do you let her get away with it? If you have sole custody and haven't been in a relationship with her for years, why not tell people the truth? Why let her play the martyr like she's the one being wronged? Like she cares about Trevor at all? She blackens your reputation repeatedly."

"I don't give a damn about my reputation. People will believe what they want to believe no matter what I say. If I deny her allegations, then that just gives her what she wants and keeps it in the news."

"What about Trevor? He's old enough to hear and see some of this. How do you think it makes him feel? Have you talked to him about it? What if he believes even a little bit that he has a mother who wants him and you're keeping him from her? Kids can be cruel. What if the kids are teasing him?"

"Is it really Trevor and my reputation you're worried about, or is it your own? Do you really care so much what complete strangers think or say about you?" He throws off the sheet, stands, and yanks on his jeans.

"Yes, it might seem silly to you, but it does bother me all those people who don't even know me will believe I'm some horrible person who shouldn't be around a child. But I *am* concerned about Trevor. Do you really think none of this fazes him at all?"

"I think he's smart enough to not care what others think."

"Oh, and I'm not smart, is that what you're saying?"

He shoots me a glare and drags his shirt over his head. "Don't put words in my mouth."

"So instead of discussing this, you're just going to leave?"

"I think it's for the best before one of us says something we regret and can't take back." He storms out of the room.

My front door slams.

Our last night together and he just left.

How am I the bad guy?

How can he care so little about what the mother of his child says about the woman he claims to love?

A tear plops on to the white sheet wrapped around my chest. The circle widens and another drops beside it.

I scrub my cheeks and clench my hands into fists.

Why is it okay for her to say anything she wants, yet I can't ask questions to understand why silence is the best course of action? It affects me, too. She's attacking me, too.

How can he not see that?

How can he just walk out on me like that?

I whip my pillow at the wall and punch the mattress.

If he really loves me, shouldn't he defend me?

Maybe I should make a statement myself about what a lying, scheming, deadbeat mother she is. Doesn't anyone fact check something before they blast it to the world? Fact: they've been divorced for years. Fact: she's never been a mother to Trevor. Fact: I had nothing to do with the end of their relationship. Fact: I am not a horrible person who shouldn't be around Trevor.

No, I can't drag any hint of Trevor into this. That would make me as bad as she is.

I hug the remaining pillow and curl into a ball.

Am I selfish and shallow because I care what people think and I want the man I love to fight back at my attackers? My family has never stood up for me, either. I guess I'm asking too much of Holden—expecting too much. I always expect too much, and then when I'm let down, I'm disappointed and upset. When will I learn?

Will I see Holden or Trevor before they leave? He wouldn't just go back to Texas without saying goodbye, would he?

Tears dampen my face and pillow. I bury my face in the pillow and scream.

I slap the mattress with both hands as I scream again. I should've known a relationship with Holden would never work. He's a gorgeous celebrity and I'm just me—the family screwup.

My raw throat aches. Snot and drool mix with the tears and drench the pillow.

Waldo whines at the side of the bed. I pat the mattress and wrap my arms around him when he lies down next to me.

Chapter Twenty

Waldo's whining drags me from sleep. Does he need to go out? What time is it? I scrunch open one eye and peer at the clock on my nightstand. One in the morning? He never needs to go out in the middle of the night.

Unless I forgot to take him out before bed—which I did because I cried myself to sleep.

I sit up and scrub my face with my fingers to wake myself up. The sheet wraps around my body like a giant, white tourniquet. I wiggle and yank until I kick myself free.

Waldo's whine comes from the other room. He must be at the front door. The poor baby. A quiet thump sounds while I drag on a pair of pants and a sweatshirt. I stick my head out of the hole in the top when Waldo's whine follows another thump.

It's too loud to be his tail. Did he knock something over—twice? I peek out the doorway of my bedroom. Waldo sits in front of the door wagging his tail. The soft thump comes again.

Somebody is at the door. Did Holden return?

I stride across the room but stop short of swinging open the door as my brain awakens enough for caution to prevail. It could be a deranged ax murder at my door instead of Holden. I peek through the hole. His blond head is bowed, but he's wearing the same clothes from earlier.

His head lifts when I open the door, and his green gaze sweeps over me. "I'm sorry. Can I come in?"

Tears threaten, and I nod. He pats Waldo on the head as he walks in, kisses me on the cheek, and pulls me into his arms.

His sheepskin coat is like ice, so I burrow my hands under the open coat and around his waist. Even his shirt is freezing. "Why are you so cold?"

"Been walking."

"All this time?" I rear my head back and inspect his face and hands. "You could catch hypothermia!"

"I'm fine."

I rub his icicle hands between mine. "Maybe we should go to the hospital. Have you lost any feeling in your fingers? Toes? I'm fairly sure that's a thing."

"Shhh...Angel, I'm fine. My hands were in my pockets most of the time."

"Hot shower. Go." I point toward my bathroom.

"We need to talk first."

"After. Whatever you need to say can wait a few more minutes until I know you're warm and not at risk for losing your extremities because you decided to take a stroll at night in the middle of winter. This isn't Texas, Holden!"

His lips twitch, and one side lifts. "There's my little spitfire."

"So help me, if you say something corny like I'm beautiful when I'm angry, I just might throw something at you."

He runs an icy finger down my cheek. "You're always beautiful. I can tell you've been crying, and I'm so sorry I caused it."

"Shower first. Talk later. I have to take Waldo out anyway." I grab his leash off the coat rack, and his tail whips back and forth.

"I'll do it."

"No, you won't. Shower."

Holden frowns. "It's dark. You shouldn't be going out there alone at this time of night."

"It's well-lit, and Waldo won't let anyone near me if I don't want them to. Go, I'll be back before you're done in the shower."

I yank on my coat, hat, and gloves before stepping outside. The cold slaps me in the face, and I hunch my shoulders. He wandered for hours in this?

I'm shivering by the time Waldo does his business and we're back inside. The fan in the bathroom drones and the water is on. Good, he listened.

My reflection in the small oval mirror by the door freezes me in my tracks. My hair is in distinct clumps all over my head. My face is sheet white except for the remnants of eye makeup smudged around my eyes and in streaks on my cheeks. I resemble a clown from a horror film.

If he can still find beauty in this, it must be love. I grab a paper towel from the kitchen and scrub my face the best I can. As I walk into the bedroom, I smooth down my hair and twist it into a bun. After wrapping a thick blanket around me, I toddle back into the living room and wedge myself in the corner of the couch.

He came back.

I drop my head and stare at the ceiling.

What is he going to say? How are we going to resolve this? Should I tell him I'll get over it and it's okay? Our relationship is more important. I don't want to fight anymore. Eventually, I will get past all the hate aimed my way. It sucks, but it's not the end of the world to have complete strangers hate and judge me based on total lies.

There aren't scandals in my past that make me dangerous to be around Trevor. She has to be making it all up. No one close to me would have anything to do with her. Even if she managed to talk to someone who knows me, there's certainly no scandal to reveal. I'm a small-town business owner, not a criminal with a shady past.

It doesn't matter. The people that matter won't believe a word coming out of her poisonous lips.

Holden walks out in a pair of low-hanging black sweats and nothing else. He must've left them here before. He dries his hair with the towel and hangs it over his neck.

"Do you want something to drink? I can make some coffee."

"I'll get it." He turns on the machine and gets a mug from the cabinet. "You want one?"

"No, thanks."

He pops in a coffee pod and places his hands on the counter in front of the machine. The kitchen window shows his reflection. He's frowning, and he appears worried.

"I shouldn't have freaked out. I'm not used to someone I don't know attacking me like that. This whole living-under-public-scrutiny thing is new to me. You're right, I shouldn't care what they think. The people who care about me won't believe any of it."

His head drops.

Is he relieved?

"It's not fair to you. You didn't choose this life. You shouldn't have to accept being attacked in the media because of your association with me." He jabs the button on the coffee maker.

What is he saying? Is he breaking up with me over this?

"Holden—"

"Hear me out, please." He turns around and grips the edges of the towel in his fists. "I was wrong to expect you to let it go and not be bothered by it."

I wrap my arms around my raised knees. He's apologizing and telling me he was wrong, but his demeanor and tone are screaming terrible news is on the way.

The whirr of the coffee machine as it finishes and the wind outside are the only sounds. Holden walks out of the kitchen without grabbing his coffee. He paces across the living room and back again. The space is only about a dozen or so feet, and with his long stride it takes him seconds. It's a bit like watching one of those old carnival shooting games where the target continuously moves in a straight line back and forth.

He suddenly stops at the end of the couch and stares at me. "What I'm about to tell you I've never told anyone before—not a single soul."

"Okay." I tuck my legs under me and sit up straight.

He rubs his hands over his face.

"Holden, what is it? You're really starting to scare me here. Are you in some kind of trouble?"

He whips the towel across the room and places his hands on the arm of the couch. His gaze pleads with me. "Swear to me you'll never repeat it to anyone, please. I'm trusting you with my life, Angel."

Good God! Did he murder someone? No, he couldn't have, not the Holden I know. Is he a criminal? Is Samantha blackmailing him?

Can I stand by him no matter what he reveals?

I rise on my knees and rest my hands on my thighs. "I swear. I love you, Holden. We'll figure it out."

His gives me a wobbly smile, and there are tears in his eyes. "I love you, too, Angel. Trevor isn't my biological son."

"What!" I grab the back of the couch as my body sways toward the floor. "I don't understand. How…no, I understand how. I mean…God!"

He collapses onto the couch and stares off across the room. "I didn't know at first—not for years. Trevor was three when I found out. We'd been battling out with the lawyers pretty much since he was born. I wanted full custody. She wanted the money train to stay open. My lawyer suggested the paternity test to rule out any contingencies. I fought it at first because I didn't see the point."

Holden drops his head to the back of the couch and stares at the ceiling. "That's not the truth. The truth is there was always a niggling doubt at the back of my mind. Samantha wasn't exactly the faithful type."

I climb across the couch, sit against his side, and take his hand. He squeezes mine.

"The lawyer set it all up and swore to keep it private. I didn't want her knowing about it and using whatever the results were as leverage."

"She doesn't know you know?"

"I'm not even sure if she knows for sure he's not mine. I think if she did, she would've bankrupted me with her demands a long time ago."

I rest my head on his shoulder. "I understand. You refute nothing she says or does because you're afraid she'll fight back and take Trevor away from you."

"Yes. I'm sorry. I know it's not fair to you."

"Don't be ridiculous. You were right. What she says doesn't matter. We have to protect Trevor. Wait, if you have full custody, she must not know, right? I mean, how does that work?"

"She gave up any rights she has to Trev, but his biological father might have a case and sue me for custody. If she knows, or finds out, she could manipulate him. I could lose my son or have to share him with a complete stranger. Maybe I'm being selfish, I don't know. His biological father could be a great guy."

"So you don't know who it is?"

"No, I checked into her past, but there's no way of knowing without digging further and risking it being exposed. I don't want to take the risk."

"No, of course not. You can't risk her or the press finding out, so you can't discover whether or not the guy is a creep. Maybe when Trevor is older, you can tell him and let him decide if he wants to dig for the identity of his biological father."

"That's my plan. When Trev turns eighteen, I'll explain everything."

"She's a horrible woman."

He snorts. "Yeah, there's not a maternal cell in her entire body. Something is broken inside her. She cares nothing for her son, only about money and fame."

"Trevor's lucky he has you."

"I'm the lucky one. I wasn't the most upstanding guy when he came along. I drank too much. Partied too much. That all changed the moment I laid eyes on him. It doesn't matter if we share the same DNA. It never did. He's my son."

Chapter Twenty-One

I dump the rest of the leftovers into the garbage. The fridge is empty of anything that will spoil before Holden and Trevor return. Watching them pack was too depressing, but cleaning out the fridge isn't much better.

My phone rings, and Franny's smiling face appears on the screen. Maybe a chat will cheer me up.

"I know you're busy this morning with Holden and Trevor leaving for Texas, but there's something I think you should know before you go into town or anywhere, really. I'm sorry, I'm not handling this well." Franny sighs loudly. "Kelly—"

"It's okay, Franny. If you're talking about Samantha's latest lies, I already know."

"Oh, okay, are you all right? Is there anything Mitch and I can do? You know you're welcome at the house any time. I'm at the bakery at the moment, but Mitch is home. He can pick you up."

"Thanks, Franny, but I'm at the cabin with Holden and Trevor. They're packing and will head to the airport in an hour or so. I'll probably crawl back into bed after that. My store is closed today, so I've got nothing to worry about."

"Why don't you come to the house and hibernate as long as you want there? I guarantee no one will bother you."

"You're the best, Franny, and if the media decides to descend again, I might take you up on that. Holden's already said I can stay here, too. Right now I just want to spend time with Holden and Trevor before they leave."

"Of course you do. I'll hang up then, but the offer is always open."

I tap the top of my phone against my forehead with my eyes closed. Saying goodbye sucks.

"Everything okay?" Holden stands in the entryway to the kitchen. He glances at my phone.

"Franny was just checking on me. She heard the news and offered for me to stay with them again."

"I wish you'd stay here at the cabin. The lake is the only exposed area, and I've got alarms wired if anyone comes on land there, too."

"Thanks, and I might if it gets crazy, but I think it would be too sad here without you and Trevor. It'll be bad enough at my place."

He strides across the kitchen and puts his hands on my hips. "Then come with us."

"What about my shop?"

"You can hire someone to manage it while you're away. We can come back whenever Trev isn't in school. You can always fly back if you have to for an emergency."

"That sounds wonderful, Holden, but I can't afford to hire someone to manage my shop in my absence. I'm not a wealthy woman. I do okay, but not enough to support a full-time manager."

"I'll pay for it."

"No, thank you, but no. I'll sell the shop. It'll take a while to handle everything. I can't just close up and leave Lenore and Patty high and dry. I have to give them time to find other jobs. I have to dispose of my inventory, and I still have orders I need to fulfill. I have bookings for the next six months."

"Or...we could do the exact opposite and move to Granite Cove." Trevor stands in the doorway with his hands in the front pockets of his jeans. There's a slight blush across his cheekbones. He shrugs. "I've got friends here. I checked out the school Timmy and Tommy go to, and it's ranked as one of the best public school systems in the state. If you insist on me attending a private school, there's one of those in town, too. Both start next week, so there's plenty of time to get me enrolled here."

Holden rubs the back of his neck and stares at the floor.

Trevor takes a few steps into the kitchen. "You already have a manager for the ranch, Dad. And we can visit Texas anytime to see everyone."

My phone rings, and I glance at it before silencing the sound. Rebecca. She probably heard the news. I shoot her a text that I'm fine and I'll call her later and shove my phone in my back pocket.

Should I say anything? My vote is definitely for Granite Cove, but I have no idea what Holden is thinking.

"Sounds like you have it all worked out." Holden places his hands on his hips and smiles at Trevor.

"It's a solid plan, Dad."

I cover my mouth with my hand to hide my grin.

Holden laughs and tugs his son in for a hug and then turns to me. "What do you think, Angel? As usual, my son is smarter than me and solved all our problems already."

"I think I'm madly in love with both of you, and I'm so happy I might burst." I stride over and envelop them both in a giant hug.

After a minute, Trevor pulls away. "I'm going to go unpack and tell my friends the good news."

"I'm surprised you bothered to pack at all. When were you going to tell me about your plan?"

"I was hoping you'd suggest it on your own, but you didn't, so I was planning on talking to you this morning. Then I figured it probably wasn't a good time because you'd be upset about Samantha's latest drama. But I overheard you talking about Kelly moving to Texas so..." Trevor shrugs.

Holden grimaces and sighs. "You heard about that, huh? I'm sorry, Trev. You want to talk about it?"

Trevor glances at me and back to his dad.

"I'm going to return some calls. You guys talk."

"No, wait." Trevor stuffs his hands back in his pockets. "You should stay. I'm sorry she said those things about you."

"Oh, Trevor, never apologize to me for what she says." I hug his shoulders. "Are you sure you don't want to talk to your dad alone?"

He shakes his head. "We're family now, right?"

Holden places his hand on Trevor's shoulder. "That's right."

"Since we're moving and sort of starting fresh and all, don't you think it's time to tell the truth about Samantha? She's never been a mother to me, and you'll always be my dad no matter what she says."

Holden rears his head back and grows pale. "Has she said something to you? When? What did she say?"

I squeeze Holden's hand. Did that awful woman say something to Trevor about Holden not being his biological son?

"I heard her shouting into the phone once a few years ago when that judge made me stay with her those few times. She said you were too stupid to figure out I wasn't even your son and if you wanted me back you would pay her for it."

Holden grabs the counter and bows his head as if his legs are too weak to hold him. I shove my shoulder under his arm and wrap my arm around his waist.

The woman is even worse than I thought. Tears fill my eyes.

"Uh, Dad...you didn't know? Oh man..." Trevor covers his mouth with his hand. His eyes are wide with horror.

Holden grabs him in a hug. "I knew. I'm so damn sorry you had to find out that way."

I grab a couple of tissues and wipe the tears off my face.

He cups Trevor's shoulders in his hands. "Why didn't you tell me?"

"I don't know. It took me awhile to understand it all. I figured you knew and that's why you let her say all that rotten stuff about you all the time because you were worried she could take me away from you."

"She can't—not anymore. She signed away any rights to you. But..." Holden sighs. "I thought we'd have this discussion when you were older. You have a biological father out there somewhere who could potentially sue for custody."

"No, I don't." Trevor shakes his head and frowns. "You don't know? He died when I was like five or six, I think. She complained about the well running dry or something. He was paying her to keep quiet about me because he had another family."

"I need to sit down." Holden folds into one of the kitchen chairs and lays his head on the table.

I squeeze Trevor tight and then rub Holden's back.

Trevor slides into the chair next to him. "You okay, Dad?"

Holden lifts his head. Tears are coursing down his face. I grab the box of tissues while my eyes fill and overflow again. I jerk a couple out and set the box in front of him.

"It's over. It's finally over." Holden puts his face in his hands as sobs shake his shoulders.

I wrap my arms around him from behind and cry against the back of his shoulder.

"I'm sorry, Dad, I thought you knew." There's a wobble in Trevor's voice.

I raise my head. Trevor's eyes are full of tears. My heart breaks, and I wrap my arms around him. "It's okay. Your dad is crying happy tears."

The burden Holden has been carrying for years has finally dissipated. No one can take his son his away from him.

Holden grabs Trevor's hand and nods. "Thank you, Son. Kelly's right. These are very happy tears." He pulls Trevor into a hug, and I grab more tissues.

Chapter Twenty-Two

The flames dance in the fireplace as the wood crackles and spits occasionally. Waldo snores in his bed on the side of the stone hearth. Holden's breaths are deep and even against my back. Every once in a while, he emits a soft puff of air and his fingers twitch on my hip.

Trevor and the twins are having a sleepover at Drew's. Rebecca called about an hour ago and said Olivia is a saint and she doesn't know how she makes parenting twins look so damn easy. She's sending Olivia flowers and a large bottle of wine. I laughed and agreed because when they had a sleepover here a couple of weeks ago, I was exhausted by dinner time.

Rebecca doesn't fool me, though. I know the real reason she called was to check on me. Franny had called earlier, too. She had been more direct and asked if I saw the latest about Samantha and if I was okay. Rebecca knows I no longer watch or care about anything to do with Samantha Fox ever since her arrest for DUI and drug possession. The video of her screaming profanity at the arresting officers and threatening to have them fired went viral. There were some who blamed her relapse on Holden filing a multimillion-dollar lawsuit against her. Others finally saw her for what she is, an evil woman and a pitiful human being. I actually felt sorry for her and what she could have had.

She could've had the love of a wonderful son, but she threw it all away.

I snuggle deeper into the pillow and Holden's arms.

He pulls me closer. "Warm enough?"

His soft drawl turns my insides into lava every time. I cover his arm with mine. "Mmm hmm. Did you have a nice nap?"

He threads our fingers together. "I was just resting my eyes."

"Uh huh. We call that a nap where I'm from."

He shifts on the couch. "This couch isn't comfortable enough for a proper nap."

"I have to agree with you there."

"It's not surprising the previous owners were happy to leave it behind when I asked for them to sell me the furnishings with the cabin."

I chuckle. "You could replace it, you know."

"I figured you do it. I assume you'll want to redecorate the place to suit your tastes."

I gawk at him over my shoulder. "Are you asking me to move in with you?"

"You're pretty much living here anyway. It makes little sense for you to keep paying rent on your place unless you really want to. Your couch is also more comfortable. We could bring that one over here."

"The romance of your invitation has me all aflutter."

He laughs and kisses my cheek. "I deserve that, I suppose." He plays with my fingers. "I thought I'd save the romance for a marriage proposal. Olivia and Luke are getting married next week, and I figured I'd pop the question then."

My mouth practically drops to the floor. "Holden Fox, you do not propose at another person's wedding! That is Olivia's special day and…"

He bursts out laughing. "I was kidding!"

I smack him with the pillow.

"Give me some credit. Do you really think I would ruin someone else's wedding or tell you what I was planning?"

I sink back down to the couch. "No."

He kisses me beneath my ear. "I do want you to move in, and I do want you to be my wife."

My breath freezes in my lungs.

His lips brush along the edge of my ear. "I want to see my ring on your finger." He trails his fingers over the back of my ring finger.

He nips the lobe of my ear between his lips. "I want you in my bed every night, and I want to wake up next to you every morning."

He kisses down the side of my neck. "I want to see your beautiful face across the table for every meal. I want to hear your tinkling laugh that gets me hard every time I hear it."

He puts his hand on my stomach. "I want to see your womb swell with our child."

I suck in a breath, and tears fill my eyes. I've turned into a regular watering pot these days.

His lips roam to my jaw. "I want to be there for you when you've had a bad day and need a shoulder to cry on or when you've had a good day and need someone to celebrate with."

I turn and cup his face in my hands.

He smiles and kisses me on the tip of my nose. "What do you say, Angel? Will you marry me? I promise I planned an entire proposal, but I don't want to wait."

I nod and plant a kiss on his lips.

"You'll have to act surprised when I propose officially because Trev has been helping me plan everything for when we go back to Texas and he'll be crushed if I don't follow through."

I nod and kiss him again.

"Have you lost the power of speech?"

I nod, and he laughs and kisses me.

"I'll choose to take that as a testament to my romantic proposal." He chuckles and kisses me again. "I love you, Angel."

"I love you so much. Sometimes I feel like it's going to explode out of my chest like confetti. I know how silly that sounds, but that's how it feels."

"I happen to like confetti."

"I don't have all the pretty words you do, but I want everything you said."

"The only pretty word I need to hear from you is yes."

"Yes. A billion times—yes!"

Epilogue

Towering pine trees line the driveway, and light posts guide the way home. Every time I drive down the driveway to the cabin, I smile because I know Holden and Trevor are waiting for me inside.

I finally found a renter to sublet my apartment because my lease isn't up for another six months, and tomorrow we all fly to Texas where Holden plans to officially propose. For Trevor's sake, maybe I should practice my surprise expression a few times in the mirror. I'll never be an actress, that's for sure. I'll leave all the acting to my future husband.

Holden is there waiting when I drive into the garage. He's done this every night since I moved in. I suppose he's a fantasy man to most, but to me he's home. A very sexy home.

He opens my door with a grin and a wink. "How was your day, Angel?" He takes my hand.

"Pretty great, actually, and even better now that I'm home with you." I kiss him. "What's for dinner? Trevor texted me you and he picked something up."

"I figured it would be fewer dishes to wash before we leave in the morning."

"Good idea."

"I have them from time to time." He opens the door to the cabin.

White lights are strung along all the beams in the ceiling. Candles flicker from every table in the room. Dozens of vases filled with pink-and-purple tulips are strewn around the room. Trevor grins in front of the fireplace with Waldo sitting at his side.

"Rebecca said tulips are your favorite, particularly pink and purple because they remind you of your time in Paris."

I nod.

Holden whispers in my ear, "Speechless again, Angel?"

I nod again.

He chuckles.

"You said Texas," I whisper back.

"I lied. I wanted you to be surprised." His lips brush my ear.

"Surprised?"

I sniffle and nod.

He takes my purse, places it on the chair, and then takes my hand and leads me across the room. "Trevor has something he'd like to show you."

"It's showtime, Waldo." Trevor makes a gesture with his hand, and Waldo bows down.

I gasp. "How did you teach him to do that? I can't even get him to sit most of the time."

"Lots of practice. I watched a video on how to do it. It's a myth you can't teach an old dog new tricks." He rubs Waldo's head. "Not that you're old, Waldo."

"He's been practicing for a couple weeks."

"I'm very impressed." I hug Trevor and pet Waldo. He leans against my leg, and something bumps against my hand.

A box with a bow dangles from his collar.

Holden gets down on one knee, removes the box from the collar, and holds it in his palm. "Kelly—"

I drop on my knees in front of him and grab his hands. "Yes!"

He bursts out laughing. "You're supposed to wait until the end of my pretty speech."

"I know, but then I'll start crying the ugly cry and my makeup will be all over my face, my throat will be raw, I'll exhaust myself, and I won't be able to fully appreciate the beauty of this moment."

Trevor clears his throat. "Does that mean we can eat now? I'm starving."

I fall into Holden's arms, laughing.

He slides a ring onto my finger. "Sure, Trev. It looks like this might be the shortest proposal in history."

I wiggle my fingers so the square-cut diamond sparkles from the firelight.

"Like it?" Holden squeezes my other hand.

"It's beautiful!"

"I told you Mom would love it. Now let's eat."

I gasp and raise my head.

Trevor stands a few feet away shifting from foot to foot. "Is that okay? If I call you Mom?"

I slap a hand over my mouth when sobs and tears overwhelm me.

"That's her way of saying yes." Holden pulls me to my feet and into his arms.

Trevor wraps his arms around me, too. "I guess you're having the ugly cry after all."

I snicker between sobs.

Holden rubs my back. "Go eat. We'll be over in a minute."

His cheek rests on top of my head. "Since you're already crying, I think now might be a good time to tell you Trev wants your name added to the official adoption, too."

I sag against his chest and picks me up in his arms and carries me to the couch. He holds me in his lap while I blubber all over him.

These pregnancy hormones are no joke. I was going to surprise him when he proposed in Texas, but he surprised me first.

I guess I can still surprise him when we get to Texas.

We'll see who's the ugly crier then.

Thank you for reading A Yearning Dilemma! If you haven't already, read the other books in the Granite Cove series:

My First My Last My Only

Covet thy Neighbor

No Choice At All

Whispers & Broken Promises

In the mood for romantic suspense? Check out Guilt & Redemption.
All my books are on my website: https://www.DeniseCarbo.com
Sign up for my newsletter to be the first to hear about new books, exclusive excerpts, sales, and giveaways: http://eepurl.com/dt5N7M

About the Author

Denise Carbo writes Romance and Women's Fiction. She is a voracious reader, loves to travel, is fascinated by the supernatural, and enjoys solving mysteries.

She lives in a small, picturesque, New England town with her high school sweetheart and their three amazing sons. Find out more at https://www.DeniseCarbo.com and sign up for her newsletter to be the first to hear about sales, giveaways, contests, and exclusive content. https://eepurl.com/dt5N7M

facebook.com/denisecarboauthor

twitter.com/DeniseCarbo

instagram.com/DeniseCarbo

Also by Denise Carbo

My First My Last My Only

Guilt & Redemption

All books listed on my website: https://www.DeniseCarbo.com

CPSIA information can be obtained
at www.ICGtesting.com
Printed in the USA
LVHW082037070123
736681LV00052B/1328